A Case of Rape

Chester Himes

A Case of
Rape

HOWARD UNIVERSITY PRESS
Washington, D.C.
1984

Printed in the United States of America

Library of Congress Cataloging in Publication Data

Himes, Chester B., 1909-
    A case of rape.

    I. Title.
PS3515.I713C3 1983   813'.54   84-3841
ISBN 0-88258-143-0

A Case of Rape

1. The Charge

*T*estimony was presented by the instruction judge to the effect that Mrs. Elizabeth Hancock Brissaud accompanied Scott Hamilton to his hotel room at three o'clock of the afternoon of Sunday, September 8th.

Mrs. Brissaud had dropped the name of her husband, André Brissaud, since divorcing him a year previously, and was known to her Paris acquaintances simply as Mrs. Hancock. She was employed in the administration offices of the American Hospital in Paris. She was a slight, trim woman with graying hair, weighing about one hundred and five pounds, and with a flair for stylish clothes.

Scott Hamilton was a tall, light-complexioned, conservative-looking, middle-aged American Negro.

Madame Maulnier, the mother of the patron, who kept a vigil in the hotel bureau every Sunday after-

3

A Case of Rape

noon while her son took his family to the country, testified that Mrs. Hancock appeared normal and composed when she arrived. Madame Maulnier had had the opportunity to see Mrs. Hancock when Scott stopped in the bureau for his key. She emphasized that she had scrutinized Mrs. Hancock carefully, as she did all white women accompanying Negro men to their rooms. She had noticed nothing in the demeanor of either to indicate they might have been quarreling. Neither appeared agitated or irate. True, their expressions were devoid of the customary fatuousness apparent on the faces of couples bent on the favorite Sunday afternoon pastime of Parisians. As a consequence, Madame Maulnier had concluded that Mrs. Hancock's visit was of a business nature.

Further testimony established that this was the first time Mrs. Hancock had ever been inside of this hotel, and that this was one of the few times she had been seen by fellow Americans in that section between the Odéon and the Panthéon known by them as "The Quarter."

The couple had come to the hotel directly from the *Café Monaco*, located on rue Monsieur le Prince a few doors from the Odéon, which was a popular hangout of Americans residing in the Quarter. Scott had arrived at the café at about a quarter past two

4

A Case of Rape

o'clock. Mrs. Hancock had joined him at two-thirty. They had sat on the terrace, conversing in low intense voices, until they had left, walking in the direction of Scott's hotel, at about five minutes to three.

During that time Mrs. Hancock had one cup of *café noir*. Scott had two beers. No witnesses were produced who had overheard any of their conversation. However, several appeared who had seen them together. They testified that she appeared in a normal state of health. There was nothing unusual about her clothing or carriage. Under cross examination they admitted she might have appeared depressed or upset, but that would not necessarily have attracted attention in the *Café Monaco*.

From this it was assumed that Mrs. Hancock was in a normal state mentally and physically when she arrived at the hotel room where she died.

Caesar Gee, the second of the defendants, arrived at the hotel alone a few minutes later. Theodore Elkins and Sheldon Edward Russell, the other defendants, arrived together five minutes later. All were American Negroes.

Madame Maulnier admitted that she noticed nothing unusual in their attitudes, unless it was the fact they were all unaccompanied by women. The three of them visited Monsieur Hamilton every Sunday

A Case of Rape

afternoon, but to her memory they had always brought women. White women, she added. All of the guests were permitted visitors in their rooms before ten o'clock, and of course she could not be held responsible for what took place behind closed doors.

During the following three hours, no untoward sound or incident attracted attention to the room.

Shortly before six o'clock, a French couple, looking from the window of a room across the court, witnessed a struggle taking place between a white woman and four Negro men.

The man, Gerard Roussel, age twenty-one, was a student in the Sorbonne.

The woman, Suzanne Bovy, age thirty-seven, occupant of the room, stated that she was an unemployed coiffeur.

Suzanne had arisen from bed and gone to the window for a breath of fresh air. Immediately she called Gerard from bed. It appeared to them as though Mrs. Hancock was trying to prevent the four Negro men from pushing her from the open window. Tears were streaming down her face. She was screaming. The witnesses were able to distinguish the words "no-no-no" and "help-help" uttered repetitiously. They heard her cry other expressions in English, which neither of them understood.

A Case of Rape

Under cross-examination they admitted that the woman and four men were fully clothed. Three of the men wore their suit coats and one a light brown sweater. The woman was dressed in a tweed skirt and a blouse. They were unable to state whether or not her clothing was torn.

Gerard shouted at the men to release the woman. One of them shouted in reply, "Go to hell!" Both of the witnesses were acquainted with the English words. Suzanne threatened to call the police, hoping thereby to cow them. One of the men closed the window and drew the curtains, and the witnesses continued to hear screams and sounds of a struggle emanating from the room. There were no telephones in the rooms, so Suzanne had to run downstairs to the bureau in order to summon the police.

Gerard dressed quickly and hastened into the hallway to the door of Scott's room. By then the sounds of screaming and struggling had ceased. Gerard heard only the murmur of low-pitched voices. His knocking went unanswered. However, he remained in the corridor outside of the door, where he was joined shortly by Suzanne, until the police arrived.

The police found Mrs. Hancock lying on the bed. Her blouse was torn and her skirt disarranged. Her girdle, which also served as a garter belt, was pulled

A Case of Rape

down about her ankles. There was a wet towel about her face and dark purple bruises on her arms. She appeared to have just died. The faces of Scott Hamilton and Sheldon Russell were scratched and bleeding. The clothing of all four men were disheveled and showed evidence of a struggle.

After preliminary questioning, the defendants were detained. The body was removed and the following day delivered to the Médecin Légiste for an autopsy.

At the request of the defense attorneys, three independent doctors had been permitted to re-examine the findings of the autopsy. One of the doctors was of French nationality, the second a French-educated Martiniquan, the third a Harvard-educated New Englander on the staff of the American Hospital in Paris, and a former acquaintance of the deceased.

The autopsy revealed that Mrs. Hancock had been sexually used at least four times within a period of twelve hours preceding her death. It could not be determined whether by the same person or different persons. Tests performed on the blood and vital organs revealed lethal traces of cantharides, a powerful aphrodisiac known as *Spanish Fly*. The aphrodisiac had been taken internally. Whether it had been administered forcibly or taken voluntarily could not be determined from the autopsy. Nor could it be determined whether it had been taken before or after her sexual employment.

The three doctors issued a statement that death was due to heart seizure resulting from the action of cantharides in the bloodstream, extravasted by physical exhaustion brought on by sexual over-indulgence.

Under cross examination it was admitted that, in view of the testimony, it was unlikely that the aphrodisiac had been taken before the victim arrived at the scene of her death. The amount found in her bloodstream would have rendered her incapable of acting rationally and walking the distance from the *Café Monaco* to the hotel on rue Cujas unassisted. The Martiniquan surgeon expressed the opinion that death had resulted within thirty minutes after the victim had taken the stimulant. The other doctors refrained from giving an opinion on this point.

Mrs. Hancock's actions of the previous night and morning, up until the time she had joined Scott Hamilton at the *Café Monaco*, had been investigated by the police.

It had been established that she had met a fellow employee, Mrs. Harriet Payne, on the terrace of the *Café de la Paix* on Place de l'Opéra at seven o'clock. They had been joined by two American businessmen, Messrs. John Barkley and Henry Thompson, with

A Case of Rape

whom they had engagements for the evening. Mr.
Barkley was driving his own car, a Cadillac sedan.
The four of them drove from the *Café de la Paix* to a
small fashionable restaurant in Montmartre where
they had dinner, and afterwards attended the *Théâtre
du Grand Guignol* on rue Chalpan near Place Pigalle.
From there they went to the *Lido* on Avenue des
Champs-Elysées, where they remained until four
o'clock a.m. Mr. Barkley then drove the ladies home;
first Mrs. Payne to an apartment house on rue de Lille
in Levallois where she rented a furnished room in
the apartment of a Russian Princess; then Mrs. Hancock to the *Hôtel Welcome*, at the corner of Saint
Germain Boulevard and rue de Seine, on the Left
Bank. He and Mr. Thompson returned to their rooms
in the *Hôtel California* on rue de Berri off Avenue des
Champs-Elysées.

The patron of *Hôtel Welcome* testified that she
had not seen Mrs. Hancock when she returned to the
hotel, nor when she left. But this was not unusual because many of the guests carried their keys at all times.

Mrs. Payne testified that Mrs. Hancock had worn
a black cocktail dress and a light straw-colored cash-
mere coat on the previous evening.

No evidence was presented to the effect she had
seen anyone between the time she returned to her

hotel and when she kept her rendezvous with Scott Hamilton at two-thirty o'clock in *Café Monaco*, which was only a three minutes walk from her hotel.

2. The Defense

The defense was conducted by a French attorney assisted by an American attorney with a consulting practice in Paris. The American attorney was prohibited by French law from pleading criminal cases in court.

The defense first presented evidence that Mrs. Hancock had formerly been the mistress of Scott Hamilton. They had met on board the *S.S. Liberté* in April of 1953. Scott had been coming to Paris for the first time. Mrs. Hancock had been returning to Dinant, Belgium, to visit her children and attempt a reconciliation with her estranged husband, André Brissaud, a dentist.

Mrs. Hancock rejoined Scott in Paris on the 14th of May. Her efforts at reconciliation with her husband had failed, and divorce proceedings had been initiated. She had lived with Scott continually until December, 1954, at which time she had returned to

A Case of Rape

the home of her aunt in Boston. During that time she had written a novel, based on personal experiences. Before returning to the U.S., as a gesture of affection, she had signed an agreement with Scott, which they had had notarized at the American Embassy in Paris, giving Scott a half interest in the work which was to be published in her name.

Scott followed Mrs. Hancock back to the U.S. at the end of January, 1955, but resided in New York.

Mrs. Hancock returned to Belgium on July 1, 1955, to spend the summer with her children. In September she returned to Paris and secured employment at the American Hospital in Paris.

Scott returned to Paris in December, 1955, arriving on Christmas Eve, and took a room in a hotel in the Fifth Arrondissement, only a short distance from the hotel where he was living at the time of Mrs. Hancock's death.

Mrs. Hancock moved into the room with him during the first week in March, 1956, and left during the last week of the following May and moved to the *Hôtel Welcome*. Scott then moved to the hotel on rue Cujas and took a cheaper room.

In July Mrs. Hancock signed a contract with an American publisher for the publication of her book, and received one thousand dollars advance royalties.

A Case of Rape

In compliance with her secret agreement, she turned over five hundred dollars to Scott.

On September 6, Mrs. Hancock received a letter from her publisher to the effect they had been informed that her book had been ghost-written by another writer, and that an agreement was in existence to this effect. If such was the case, she had committed fraud by signing the contract which contained a warranty to the effect the book was exclusively her own. Under such conditions, they could not undertake its publication. They requested that she present them with a notarized statement by herself and Scott Hamilton, denying the existence of an agreement of co-authorship, and declaring the work to be her own.

Scott testified that she had telephoned him and informed him of the letter, and had requested him to sign the statement with her. He had acceded to her request, but since he would have been out of the city all day Saturday he had made an appointment with her for Sunday at two-thirty.

When they met he learned that Mrs. Hancock believed he had written her publisher, giving the information of his half-interest in the book. He had denied this passionately, knowing how much publication of the book meant to her. She believed that only its success would enable her to have the means of having her children with her during their summer vacations.

Scott declared that he had been deeply hurt that she suspected him of writing her publisher. He wished greatly to prove to her that he had done nothing to her detriment since they had separated. As a consequence he had requested her to accompany him to his room so that he might prove by his three closest friends that he was telling the truth. She was reluctant to discuss their relationship with persons who were practically strangers to her, but he had overcome her objections by pleading for an opportunity to defend his integrity.

His friends, the three other defendants, had supported his contention. They had persuaded Mrs. Hancock that it was no doubt one of her own acquaintances, perhaps someone employed with her at the American Hospital, to whom she had let slip the information, who had written her publisher out of envy.

As was customary in a gathering of American Negroes and white persons, a discussion of interracial relations had developed. Scott's friends were witty and charming, and related, with disarming frankness, such anecdotes of racial abuse, both real and imagined, which white Americans find so fascinating. Mrs. Hancock had relaxed and had enjoyed herself. Their customary bridge game had been neglected.

A Case of Rape

The men had been drinking Scotch whiskey highballs, but Mrs. Hancock had preferred the sherry Scott had offered her.

The three other defendants had been expecting their women friends at six-thirty. Scott had urged Mrs. Hancock to wait until they arrived and accompany him to dinner. He had suggested they go to a Turkish restaurant on rue de la Huchette, which was famous for its couscous. She had consented.

Scott had played some tape recordings of Bach and Mozart.

Mrs. Hancock had drunk more than she had realized and had confessed, laughingly, that her head was spinning. Scott had persuaded her to lie down. He had covered her with a quilt and she had slept.

She had awakened at about five-thirty, and had remarked that it was close in the room. Scott had opened the window to clear out the cigaret smoke. While he was thus engaged, Mrs. Hancock had poured for herself another glass of sherry. In so doing, she had poured from a bottle in which Scott had a solution of Spanish Fly and sherry which was identical to the bottle from which she had previously been served.

Within a very short time she had become mentally deranged. She had torn her clothes and screamed and had tried to jump out of the window. The defendants

15

had restrained her forcibly and had administered first-aid treatment. They had removed her girdle which appeared to restrict her breathing, put cold wet towels about her head, and forcibly held her in bed. They all had realized she had drunk from the wrong bottle, but none of them thought it would prove fatal. While they were thus engaged, waiting for the spasm to pass, she had gasped and died.

3. The Summations

The prosecution contended that Mrs. Hancock had accompanied Scott to his room on a purely business matter. She had done so only to have Scott correct a statement which would prove injurious to herself. Whether or not Scott had written to her publisher, himself, was of no importance. If Scott had truly desired to sign jointly a statement with Mrs. Hancock to the effect that he had not contributed to the writing of her book, it could have been settled definitely during the half hour they conversed at the *Café Monaco*. His declaration that he wished to defend his integrity to Mrs. Hancock by having her talk to his

A Case of Rape

friends was childish and insincere. Obviously, from the start, his purpose had been to avoid issuing any such statement. Therefore, to render Mrs. Hancock incapable of pursuing her request, and to humiliate her in such a manner as to make her defenseless against his purposes, he had given her a glass of sherry containing the cantharides upon entering his room. Subsequently, during the period of her uncontrollable sexual excitement, all four defendants had violated her sexually, producing the state of physical exhaustion that caused her death. If such was not their premeditated purpose and intention, why had not the defendants been accompanied by their women friends as was their custom?

That the aphrodisiac had been given her without her knowledge was indisputable. That the two existing and identical bottles had been within reach of her hand for more than an hour, without her having noticed and commented upon it, was an unacceptable connotation on human behavior. She was employed by the American Hospital. She would be cognizant of the effects of such a stimulant. Even had she not been aware of its lethal nature, no white woman of her proven character would of her own volition take an aphrodisiac for the purpose of submitting sexually to four Negro men consecutively. It was asking too

A Case of Rape

much sufferance from the logic and integrity of the court to assume that the victim had taken the aphrodisiac *after* having been sexually employed by the four defendants. Of the fact she had been sexually employed by the defendants, there was no doubt. Existing evidence pointed to this conclusively.

The aforesaid being so, rape had been committed, since legally, the administration of a drug which renders the victim incapable of exercising personal volition is coincidental with the application of force. Therefore, Mrs. Hancock's death resulting from these commissions by the defendants, must be construed as premeditated murder.

The defense contended that it had been proven that Mrs. Hancock went to the room of Scott Hamilton of her own volition; it had been proven and accepted that when she had left the *Café Monaco* in the company of Scott Hamilton she had been mentally acute and physically normal.

Therefore, the entire case rested upon the presumption of what had happened *after* she had left the *Café Monaco*.

There had been nothing in Scott's attitude to arouse her suspicions. On the contrary, her very actions were evidence of her trust. She had lived with him inti-

A Case of Rape

mately for a period of more than two years. Her un-
questionable intelligence was proof that she had
known all of the traits of his character to the extent
that she entertained not the slightest fear that he
would cause her physical injury. Had he harbored
such sinister intention, she would have readily divined
it. Consequently, it must be assumed that he had no
such intention in mind.

The fact that the three other defendants had not
brought women friends with them, as was their custom, was indisputably a coincidence. Their engagement had been made on the previous Sunday. It had
been arranged at that time that they would join the
men at six-thirty o'clock. Scott did not hear from
Mrs. Hancock until the following Thursday. Therefore, any accusation of premeditation in this respect,
would have no relevance to the facts.

All four defendants had concurred in their testimony that the aphrodisiac had been taken accidentally
by Mrs. Hancock. There had been nothing in the
evidence presented to the court to raise the slightest
doubt of this contention. On the other hand, the evidence fully substantiated it. Mrs. Hancock had been
drinking sherry from a bottle that was labeled
SHERRY. She had become dizzy and had slept for a
time. She had awakened in a confused state of mind,

A Case of Rape

as is perfectly normal when one has drunk an abundance of sherry. She complained of the closeness of the air in the room. While the defendant whose room it was had been opening the window, she had served herself another drink of sherry. This had come from a bottle identical with the first, bearing an identical label. The only one of the defendants who might have readily differentiated between the two bottles had had his back turned to her, and had not seen the action.

The defendant has admitted possession of the drug. He has testified that a small bottle of this aphrodisiac, known to him as Spanish Fly, had been given to him by a white American journalist who had been returning home, who had laughingly suggested that he employ it to perpetuate one of the great American myths; and subsequently the defendant had mixed it with some sherry in a *SHERRY* bottle. He is horrified and stricken with guilt that his possession of this drug has led to the death of Mrs. Hancock, who had always maintained his highest admiration. But this does not indicate intention. This does not constitute murder. On the contrary, this supports the contention that Mrs. Hancock's death was accidental.

Nothing in the evidence supported the prosecution's claim that the victim had taken the aphrodisiac

A Case of Rape

before committing the sexual acts. No connection had been established between Mrs. Hancock's consuming the aphrodisiac and her commission of several sexual acts. (This brought a murmur of laughter from the spectators.) The medical testimony had not specified the order of their occurrence. In fact, the defense pointed out, the medical testimony established the fact that the commission of the several sex acts might conceivably have occurred previous to the consuming of the aphrodisiac. (This brought a louder laugh.)

The defense recalled that one of the distinguished surgeons who had performed the autopsy on the body had given his considered opinion that death had occurred within a maximum of thirty minutes after the victim had taken the drug. The prosecution had appealed to the integrity and logic of the court; but could there be any integrity in a logic that would assume sexual violations by four whiskey-drinking men being consummated within the time of thirty minutes?

In conclusion, the defense stated: "The prosecution has maintained that no white woman of Mrs. Hancock's character would voluntarily submit to four Negro men, three of whom were strangers. It is easy enough for all of us to concur in this assumption,

A Case of Rape

the four defendants included. But what evidence has been offered that she did submit to the defendants? Are they the only four sexually potent men in the city of Paris? Are the defendants being tried because they are Negroes and Mrs. Hancock was white? The questions here are whether or not Mrs. Hancock was raped by the defendants, and whether or not the drug was administered to her intentionally. The evidence presented here establishes beyond all doubt that the answers to both questions are *NO!*"

The prosecution concluded its argument with the blunt statement that the evidence established the guilt of the defendants beyond all reasonable doubt.

"Behind the emotional rhetoric of the defense lie these four salient facts:

"(1) Mrs. Hancock was given an overdose of a lethal aphrodisiac, cantharides, known as *Spanish Fly;*

"(2) Mrs. Hancock had been sexually employed four, or more times, shortly before her death;

"(3) These events had taken place, in accordance with all interpretations of the evidence, *after* (even the defense admits this) Mrs. Hancock arrived at the hotel room occupied by the defendant, Scott Hamilton;

"(4) These two factors, and only these, caused her

death as surely as though the defendants had bludgeoned her to death.

"It is not the obligation of the prosecution in this case, where the facts are so clear and the evidence so conclusive, to present the defendants with a motive. It is legally apparent that rape and murder have been committed, committed by these four defendants, for whatever motive. However, in that uncharted wilderness—that dark pathology of lust and hate—of interracial motivation, innumerable motives could be found."

4. The Verdict

The court returned a verdict of guilty on both counts.

5. The Sentence

The death penalty, customary but not mandatory in such cases, was deferred because of the racial origin and nationality of the defendants. They were sentenced to life imprisonment.

6. The Fourth Estate

Due to the sensational nature of the trial and the chilling reaction to the verdict, the case was given extra-ordinary attention in the press of all the nations of the world. It was presented with an attention to detail usually manifested in a declaration of war. The case histories of all five persons presented them as adult, intelligent, cultured, controlled, and moral in the acceptable connotation of the word. According to the press, neither the victim nor any of the defendants had ever exhibited, as far as was ascertained, any symptoms of criminal impulses or tendencies toward sadism, masochism or nymphomania.

However, the majority consensus of opinion supported the verdict of their guilt. Even persons considered fair-minded, and social-conscious persons who always sympathized with the under-dog, those who actually identified racially and culturally, along with the

A Case of Rape

mass of Europeans who had become deeply concerned by the invasion of race prejudice in the American manner, could find no fault with the verdict.

Four American Negro men had been caught in a room with a white woman who had died from the combined effects of an over-dose of an aphrodisiac and repeated sexual employment. In the minds of most of the people of this civilized world, they had been guilty since the banishment of Ham, the second son of Noah.

But there was scarcely any comment on the question of their guilt.

There was a total absence of editorial opinion in the French press. The facts spoke for themselves.

The English press editorialized on the tragedy of persons of Negro heritage who find themselves enclosed in an alien European culture.

The American press observed that this should prove a lesson to American Negroes running off to Europe, and advised them to return to the United States where their true friends could be found.

The Soviet press termed the trial an outstanding example of the violation of human rights in a capitalistic society, and explored all of its political implications, employing it as another propaganda horse in the East-West struggle for the minds of the colored world.

A Case of Rape

However, the justice of the verdict was not challenged.

The press of the Republic of China released a blast toward the brutalities of imperialism, including the crime, the trial and the verdict in its condemnation.

The South African white press commended the verdict while deploring the leniency of the sentence, which should have been death.

The press of West Germany remained as devoid of comment as did the French press.

The East Indian press insisted that there were no racial aspects attributive to the case, but merely a question of whether four beastly men had murdered a low woman, which had been decided by the just process of court trial.

Numerous Africans, writing individually, cited the severity of the sentence as evidence of growing racism in France. There was a remarkable unanimity in their contentions that, in cases involving whites only, death resulting from sexual violations in the French capital had been so common as to have attained the legal construction of death by natural causes.

Only the American Negro press raised doubts of the defendants' guilt. But this did not arise from the manner in which the trial had been conducted nor from lack of evidence to support the verdict. It was the natural reaction of American Negroes to suspect all justice rendered by whites.

7. The Investigator

An American Negro writer, Roger Garrison, who, with his white wife and children, had been residing in Paris since the end of the war, decided to make an investigation into the lives of the defendants. He saw in the verdict a perfect example of the racist-political ends served by all such convictions of Negro men for raping white women.

According to his considered opinion, the very essence of the trial was that of an inquisition to re-establish the inferiority of the entire Negro race. The trial had been conducted in the same atmosphere of racism that has been prevalent throughout the U.S. South since the civil war, but had only found its way into French politics on the heels of France's setbacks in Indo-China and Morocco. At the time France was engaged in a hopeless war against Algerian national-ists, a war which France dared not win, could not afford to lose, and realized there were no grounds for a peaceful settlement. Racism had bloomed in the

A Case of Rape

political pessimism, manpower depletion, over-taxation, like an odious weed. To make matters worse, Egyptian President Nasser had nationalized the Suez Canal, depriving France of a source of sorely needed revenue, and threatening the supply of oil. And France was frustrated in her desire to join England in waging war against the insolent black dictator by the lack of American participation. Therefore, second only to Frenchmen's antagonism toward rebellious blacks was their antagonism toward the lukewarm American whites; both of which antagonisms, he felt, were politically served by the conviction of four American black men for raping an American white woman.

Roger was convinced that by relating these political trends of racism to the reality of the verdict, he could prove, beyond all doubt, the international conspiracy of racism which employed convictions of rape against Negro men to maintain the Negro race in subjugation and social inferiority in much the same manner as carefully designed and premeditated pogroms had been used against the Jews.

In this investigation, Roger was not concerned with attempting to prove the innocence of the defendants. Whether they were guilty or innocent was irrelevant to the fact of their conviction. They had been convicted to prove that Negroes are an inferior race, and the task before him was to prove that the four Negro defendants were certainly not inferior persons.

He believed that from the summations of their life histories, he could present facts to prove conclusively they were unlikely types to have committed such a crime, perhaps as unlikely to have committed an act of rape as a Prime Minister of England. That was the essential question; are there in this world such Negro men so unlikely to commit the crime of rape as to make such a charge against them as absurd and ridiculous as it would appear against a Prime Minister of England?

To prove that such Negro men existed, that facts supported their existence, that they existed in such numbers as to make them as immune against such a charge as are an incalculable number of white men—that was the point. Not to prove that these particular four convicted men were any more or less guilty or innocent than four white men of comparable culture in the given situation; that had already been proven by innumerable social studies. Roger wondered if, during the entire history of France, four comparably cultured white Frenchmen had been similarly convicted of rape.

In a larger sense, Roger hoped to prove by his in-

A Case of Rape

vestigation, that the personal destinies of all black men living in a white culture were promoted and restricted with the deliberate purpose of maintaining and strengthening the assumption of Negroes' racial inferiority; that the true stature of Negroes in any field of endeavor could not be determined from what they had accomplished, but only from what they had been permitted to accomplish; that in all instances their statures were accorded to support the contentions of their racial inferiority; that the virtues of Negroes were never determined from the true nature of their motives, but only from the construction placed upon their motives for racist expediency; that their vices were never presented in the framework of good and evil, but only in their application to the opinion of whites in their judgments of blacks. Therefore, this verdict of guilty arrived at by a French court in Paris did not in reality constitute a conviction of four Negro men of the crime of rape, but presented a political conclusion by the French Republic, identical to that prevailing in the American South, that all Negro men were potential rapists.

To this end, Roger had a personal stake. He could identify with the defendants, and by their conviction on this charge, his own position became untenable.

He had been born on an Alabama cotton plantation,

A Case of Rape

one of twelve children of poverty-stricken Negro sharecroppers. He had received but the minimum of formal education in a dilapidated, over-crowded, segregated country school when, at the age of fifteen, he had gone to Harlem to live with relatives.

He had become a member of the communist party; and had been encouraged to write accounts of his experiences for the purpose of communist propaganda. His first four novels had been published by a communist press, the fifth by a famous conservative publishing house. Thereupon, prodded by both the communists and his publishers, he had written his autobiography, as do most American Negro writers. This had been hailed as a major work of art; he had been heralded a genius and catapulted to fame. But he had been imprisoned by his own success, fettered by his own honesty. By the same token which American culture had accorded him fame, American society demanded he conform.

Feverish with a desire for both personal and creative freedom, for a culture free of racial bias in which to develop his talent, for a mode of living unencumbered by the bourgeois pretentiousness of both Negro and white middle-class Americans into which he found himself suddenly projected, he had divorced his Negro wife, moved to Paris, married the French secretary

A Case of Rape

of his European literary agent, and established residence in France. Subsequently he resigned from the communist party and attacked it with the furious emotionalism that can only be experienced by a former convert.

As a consequence, he was also hailed by the rightist press and literary circles in France as the great genius of his race. It was not until his usefulness had passed and he had been dropped that he fully understood his position as a political figure. But he still remained as much a political figure as a failure as he had as a success; because as a failure he demonstrated the inferiority of his race as much as he had as a success.

Roger hoped that by proving the verdict against the four Negro defendants to be a political expediency, he might also establish that his own fame and failure had been promoted for the same purpose.

To accomplish this required great soul searching and demanded an intellectual honesty of which heretofore he had been incapable. In the United States he had been used to set the standard for the Negro superintellectual; to establish the yardstick for measuring Negro mental capacity. He had come from the very poor and oppressed. He lacked a formal education. His reasoning was emotional. His nature demanded the control and discipline of an absolute,

A Case of Rape

hence his becoming a communist. As a yardstick for Negro intellectual capacity, he served two purposes: (1) To restrict the evaluations of college-educated, culturally reared Negro intellectuals within the confines of his own mental limitations; (2) To create a Negro success story of such singular aspect as to withstand duplication, yet at the same time demonstrate it can happen. Once these ideas had been sufficiently compounded into the national race consciousness, there was no further need to be concerned about the intellectual aspirations of Negroes. Obviously, there was no Negro mind to compare with Roger Garrison's, and God knows one black genius in a nation of only one hundred and eighty million people was enough. But the opportunity remained; every Negro had a chance of being another Roger Garrison.

On the other hand, he had been used by the French, first, to illustrate their freedom from racial bias and preconceptions and, secondly, to focus public attention on America's brutal persecution of its Negro minority. The French, with their vast colonial empire in Africa, sat back and laughed sly at the American's discomfiture.

Consequently, his American supporters turned on Roger and denied him. This rendered him useless to the French, so they dropped him. In the United States, less talented writers were acclaimed as his superiors for the sole purpose of debasing him.

But as a failure, he served both nations equally and to the same end, to demonstrate that Negro mentality was limited. The proof of Roger's development was the fact he understood this. He was released from his ambition to become a French bourgeois intellectual. He mastered his shame at being identified as the protagonist of his autobiography. He knew that he had been used as a political figure to contain the claim of inferiority accorded his race, and now he wished the world to know it. He wanted his work to be evaluated on merit; he wanted to assume his true position among the writers of the world. No doubt this was his major motive for conducting the investigation. But he also knew, but for the grace of God, he could have been convicted of rape and murder too.

8. The Investigation

At the outset, Roger noticed some curious facts about the names of the persons involved.

A Case of Rape

Scott Hamilton and Elizabeth Hancock bore the family names of great American patriots, despite the fact that one was Negro and the other white.

The three defendants who had some white ancestors all bore names traceable to English origin: Scott Hamilton, Theodore Elkins, Sheldon Edward Russell.

The fourth defendant of unmixed African descent, had a name that was commonly used as a command in guiding teams without reins. *Gee* directed the team to the right; *haw* to the left. Negro slaves had used the commands when plowing. Farm hands the country over still commanded their teams in such manner. There was scarcely a mule in all of the United States that did not know *gee* from *haw*. Was it a joke, Roger wondered, played on some unsuspecting slave by a practical joker? And what kind of parents did he have who perpetuated the joke by the addition of *Caesar?*

CAESAR GEE

Caesar Gee was twenty-nine years old, small, dapper and black. He affected the drooping mustache of

35

A Case of Rape

Attila the Hun, which had been popularized by the ancient conqueror's reincarnation in color-films, along with the chin-strap beard which has become emblematic of the cult devoted to freedom of love in the *Quartier Latin*.

He was born in Tulsa, Oklahoma, where his parents, Rufus and Emma Gee, had run a liquor joint during the prohibition era. He had two sisters, one older than himself, and no brothers.

His parents had moved to Los Angeles when the sale of whiskey had again become legal, and his father had made a fortune in the *numbers* racket. There was nothing in the pattern of their lives or characters to set them apart from the majority of Negroes descended entirely from the African slaves who had tilled the land.

Caesar had grown up in Los Angeles in the lap of a vulgar sort of luxury. He had possessed all of the clothes, cars and women he desired. He had attended Jefferson High School, where for one year he had been the star of the track team.

He had been too young to see service in the war, but had served two years in the army, from 1948 until 1950, stationed at Fort Huachuca, only eight hours distant by his Olds convertible from Los Angeles Central Avenue, the heart of the colored section.

A Case of Rape

Soon after his release from the army, he had become acquainted with a middle aged, French-born white woman employed as an "expert" on period costumes by one of the major motion picture studios. This acquaintance had resulted from his running into her car. He had leaped from his car, extended his card and offered immediately to pay the cost of the damages and take her for a medical examination if she thought it necessary. She was so astounded by his polite manners and charming personality she decided instantly to take him as a lover.

For years he had been painting little obscene pictures to shock his friends. But it remained for the inherited perceptions of Madame Boutette, deriving from her background of centuries old culture, to encourage the development of his talent. At her suggestion he had come to Paris in the Fall of 1952.

Caesar Gee brought a yellow Cadillac convertible to Paris and resided for his first six months in the *Hôtel George V*. He soon learned the spoken French language from the many lovely French women he met in the fashionable cafés on the Avenue Champs-Elysées, and he made many friends among the Parisian night-life habitués and American Negro entertainers. He avoided American white people, who persisted in

37

A Case of Rape

treating him as an object of ridicule. This antipathy
finally caused him to abandon the flashy luxury of the
George V, which appealed so strongly to his nature;
and he moved into a small, dark, shockingly expensive
apartment on the Left Bank. It was in the building
next to the *Académie* of Raymon Duncan, that individual who began life as the humble brother of the
great American dancer, Isadora Duncan, and rose to
become the leading prophet, even to the flowing
white robes from the temples of ancient Greece and
a flowing white beard which would have been the
envy of Moses, of a cult which appealed tremendously
to the aestheticism of the ugliest of the international
titled leisure class.

Caesar soon discovered that his yellow Cadillac
convertible was overshadowed by appearances of bro-
cade-upholstered Rolls Royces, morning suited Empire gentlemen, the monocled noblemen and their
ladies, assisted by purblind flunkies to whom French
citizens were as invisible as American Negroes. But
when the Duke and Duchess of Windsor stopped
dead in their tracks in the middle of the street in front
of the Duncan Académie, where they were headed,
and with slow deliberation put on their spectacles,
either to identify the car, or Caesar Gee himself, who

38

A Case of Rape

at the time was in it, that was the last indignity. Furthermore, it was difficult to manage in the narrow, crowded streets of the "old city," and Caesar's conquests were not dependent on it, as long as Caesar had himself.

The Cadillac was sold and its place was taken by a Borzoi puppy with a pedigree dating from the monarchy. It belonged to the "P" limb of the Borzoi tree and Caesar named it "*Pernod.*" In six months time it had grown into a horse of a dog and in Caesar's small dark apartment took on the aspects of a monster in a dungeon. However, outside in the daylight, coal-black Caesar being dragged down the streets by snow-white Pernod was a sight to inspire awe in the hearts of even the most blasé Parisians.

Of the four defendants, Caesar was the only one who had great success with French women. He was not only loved for his money, but for himself. Some women wished to give him money. And there were others, with titles and affluence, of the highest society in Europe, who invited him to their villas on the *Cote d'Azur* and lounged with him on the hot sandy beaches, watching in silent fascination as he meticulously applied perfumed creams and sun lotions to his smooth black skin.

39

A Case of Rape

On the whole, Caesar liked ripe women on the flamboyant side, yet young enough to fill their skins with the charm of unwrinkled flesh. He had no taste for undernourished women, nervous women, flabby women, unhappy women, but he could tolerate intelligent women if they could hide their intelligence sufficiently.

During his four years residence in Paris, between the demands put upon him by his dog and his women, and his extensive travels about the continent of Europe, he found a little time to produce a stack of surrealistic paintings in colors of a rare violence. His subjects were devoted entirely to sex, revealing frankly, without shame or apology, his preoccupation with this theme. There was a canvas of black and white lesbians making love; another depicting a nude woman bending over to stare suggestively between the arch of her outspread legs; and twelve studies on variations of the sex act. All had been painted from life. Caesar had no difficulty finding models to pose for him.

From these facts, Roger Garrison concluded that Caesar Gee was more likely to have been raped than to have committed rape. But would white people agree?

A Case of Rape

SHELDON EDWARD RUSSELL

Sheldon Edward Russell, known to his friends as "Shelly," was thirty-five years old, divorced and unattached. He was a big man with an impressive build, clean-shaven, revealing a mottled-brown skin and features of a curious mixture of white and Negro lineaments, as if the bloodstreams of his forebears waged a continuous battle for domination of his face. Nevertheless, he was handsome. His black wavy hair was gray at the temples, giving him an air of distinction.

Equipped with such basic qualifications, he could be no less than a tweedy, pipe-smoking sophisticate. He impressed women as appearing exceptionally virile and had great sex appeal. But he showed none of the excitability usually attendant to this. He always appeared calm and relaxed, slowly puffing his masculine pipe and listening attentively with a twinkle in his clear brown eyes and a slight smile on his thin caucasian lips, indicative of a tolerant and humorous nature. He impressed everyone by his excellent sense of humor. He was a superb story teller, genuinely witty, and a preferable companion on all occasions.

Everyone liked him. He was the most popular American man, white or colored, then living in the

A Case of Rape

Latin Quarter. There was never a lack of women who wished to date him. His preference in women were, in this order: Swedish, English and American. On the whole he preferred big women. Beauty was secondary; intelligence preferable, charm desirable, wit unnecessary, and age of no importance.

When in Paris, Shelly held court nightly in the *Café Tournon*, located on rue Tournon across the street from the entrance to the *Palais du Luxembourg*. He was always surrounded by admirers of both sexes who wished to be entertained. Usually, from the women who were present, he made his selection for that night. Only rarely did he make dates in advance.

Although Shelly had been in Europe for three years, most of which had been spent in Paris, he spoke only a passable French, and had no desire to speak better. He spent most of his time with other Americans and English-speaking Europeans and had little occasion to speak French other than of a functional nature. He had been amazingly unsuccessful with French women, for reasons which he had never divulged, and French culture had made very little impression on his way of life.

This was due to the fact that Shelly had a tremendous pride in his own heritage. He rebelled against becoming an anonymous black person in French civilization, such as anonymous Arabs and Africans. He felt that he was a paying guest of the French Republic and wanted to be treated as one.

Shelly's father, George Bernard Russell, had been a famous militant editor of a great Negro weekly newspaper in the United States. Black, with grizzly hair and Semitic features, arrogant, fiery, egocentric, he had been both feared and revered as an outspoken advocate of racial equality.

His grandfather had been a bishop in the African Methodist Episcopal Church of America. Strange, his name had been Abraham Isaac Russell.

Bishop Russell's father, Shelley's great-grandfather, had owned a livery stable in Philadelphia from 1847 until the end of the civil war. He had been born free of slave parents who had escaped from slavery via the Underground Railway during the war of 1812.

Shelly's father, George Bernard, the militant editor, had graduated from *Hampton Institute*, in Virginia; and his grandfather from *Wilberforce College*, in Ohio.

Shelly's mother was the daughter of a white Presbyterian missionary and an American Indian girl. She had graduated from the Conservatoire of Music of Oberlin College, in Ohio, where a few colored people from all over the world attended, majoring in composition. Afterwards she taught music in the Negro college, Hampton Institute, where she met his father during a class reunion.

Shelly's father enrolled him in Harvard University, and then died of a heart seizure before Shelly had finished his first year. He continued his studies, but sick with fear and insecurity, intolerably frustrated and humiliated by the polite exclusion and exquisite scorn to which Negro students are subjected at Harvard, he married a white girl in retaliation, one Anne Bentley, daughter of an automobile dealer in Madison, Wisconsin. Anne was a sophomore at the nearby college for women, Radcliffe. A month later, at the beginning of their summer vacations, they separated, Shelly to return to his home in Philadelphia, Anne to her parents in Wisconsin, never to return. Anne's parents had the marriage annulled on the grounds that Shelly was of an alien and incompatible race.

America entered the war the following December and Shelly got an assignment as a war correspondent for the newspaper his father had edited, and spent the next three years reporting on Negro troops in the war in the Pacific. At the end of 1945 he returned to Philadelphia with a tall, big-bodied, blonde Australian wife, who had been connected with the Red Cross headquarters in Alaska.

A Case of Rape

He re-entered Harvard University and in three years received his B.A. degree in journalism. During that time he lived with his wife in Boston. After graduation he returned to Philadelphia and went to work on the editorial staff of the newspaper. His wife fell in love with a fellow employee, Ralph Baker, a man who was bigger and blacker and seemingly more virile than Shelly. They were divorced and she married Baker.

Shelly moved back to Boston and took charge of the newspaper's office there, and began writing a weekly column. He was given a wide latitude of subject matter—art, politics, gossip—providing it was interesting. He discovered a great talent for that type of journalism, and his column was an immediate success.

He met and fell in love with a white Boston socialite, a beautiful and charming woman, member of the DAR, who had recently divorced her husband, a sixty-three year old millionaire shipping magnate, also descendant from a very old Boston family, on the grounds that he was sterile and she wanted a child.

For two years Shelly lived with her on her estate in Northampton, Massachusetts. They had a child, a son, who appeared to be entirely white. When the child became a year and a half old, and showed no

A Case of Rape

indications of Negro ancestry, she ended her affair with Shelly, dismissed him from her estate, and re-married her former husband. He accepted the child who had been sired by Shelly as his own son and heir.

Shelly had loved the woman and it almost broke him. He fled to Paris and tried to lose himself in the endless concupiscence for which he had become noted in the Latin Quarter. Yet he could not get over her, could not forget her. Despite her treatment of him, he still maintained a reverence for her tradition, her social position, her heritage, her social graces, for all of her attributes of upper class, rich, white, cultured Americanisms which she possessed.

As a consequence, he had a sort of reverence for all women who were her prototypes.

He lived on the $75. weekly salary paid him by the newspaper for his column. Yet he longed to be a big syndicated columnist, earning $50,000. a year, so he could engender the admiration and respect of such upperclass women.

He longed to be a big man in any respect. But in his heart he knew he was a little man. Other people knew it too. All of the women he had ever admired and wanted to keep had learned it from the beginning of their intimacy.

He had black moods when he felt bitter and de-

A Case of Rape

feated and reveled in self-pity. But none of his acquaintances knew of these, and only the most intelligent of his mistresses. He lived in constant dread of people discovering what he really was. With studied deliberation he erected a facade of contentment and self-assurance. He was generous and helpful, especially to American white people of importance. He was considerate of upperclass American white women to the point of embarrassment. He felt contempt for other negroes, but tolerated them for their usefulness. He envied Roger Garrison for his position of importance, but toadied to him.

In a manner of speaking, Shelly Russell was a kind of dilettante *Uncle Tom*.

There are the professional *Uncle Toms* who employ it to great profit.

There are born *Uncle Toms* who have never learned any other way of relating their lives to white people than by means of *Uncle Tomism*.

There are made *Uncle Toms* who, though abhorring it, have been forced to become *Uncle Toms* in order to earn a living.

But Shelly was none of these. Shelly was the kind of *Uncle Tom* who did it for free, to have the good will and personal liking of cultured and intelligent white people, preferably of the upperclass.

47

A Case of Rape

THEODORE ELKINS

Ted Elkins was twenty-four years old, the youngest of the defendants. He had a tall, slender but well-proportioned build, and carried himself with an erectness that betokened a rare race-conscious dignity or else an abnormal self-esteem. His face was somewhat longish and his features bold, but softly rounded and exotically molded. His head was well shaped and he wore his thick, kinky hair clipped evenly about an inch in length and brushed forward. His hair was amazingly soft to the touch and had a natural sheen, which is rare in kinky hair, it usually appearing rusty. He had large brown eyes of the liquid intensity of a doe's, fringed with long black lashes. His complexion was a genuine sepia and his skin smooth and hairless.

He was always well dressed in English tailored suits, conservative and ever-so-slightly effeminate. His manner was aloof, seemingly reserved, with a suggestion of contemptuousness. He was instantly resentful of personal affront, acutely sensitive to ridicule, with the insolent intolerance for all opinions contrary to his own, denoting the self-preoccupation and immaturity to be found in students of all races and all nations.

A Case of Rape

Europeans of both sexes considered him beautiful. Parisians assumed him to be of Senagalese extraction with a dash of French blood dating from several generations back. To an extent this was true.

His great-grandfather had been brought to the United States by a somewhat nervous pirate known as Chancellement Dupré, who had stolen him from his tribe in what is now Senegal because of his impressive and handsome physique. It was Dupré's intention to retire from the risky business of pirating, settle on a plantation outside of New Orleans, and devote his remaining years to the breeding of a superior quality of giant slaves.

Dupré's project was doomed to failure by the fact that before he had arrived at his destination the South had lost the civil war and the slaves had been freed. However, his Senegalese prisoner did not know this. Dupré had scarcely time to enjoy a few days of connubial bliss with his New Orleans wife before his Senegalese treasure committed suicide with the short chain of his manacles, a feat that elicited awe in Dupré's acquaintances. However, not before his wife had managed to become impregnated by the beautiful savage.

Dupré did not discover this latter fact until months later when his wife presented him with a chocolate brown son. Dupré killed his wife, which the local authorities deemed forgivable under the circumstances. However, he kept the infant as a souvenir, giving it his own name and a Catholic upbringing.

When the younger Dupré was nineteen, he killed his father in revenge for a whipping he had received and fled to Haiti, taking the name of Edward Elkins which he saw written on a shipment of cargo in the ship's hold where he had stowed away. Twelve years later, as Edward Elkins, he returned to New Orleans' *Latin Quarter*, bringing a wife of unmixed Negro ancestry and three black children.

Ted's father, Sidney, was the second of eight additional children born in New Orleans.

Sidney became an ironworker of great skill and married a beautiful creole Negro woman whose father was unknown, a situation not unusual among creole Negroes born before the first world war.

Ted was the eldest of five children born in New Orleans. In 1937, at the height of the depression, when he was five, his father moved to Chicago and managed to get a job in a factory producing farm machinery.

Ted grew up in Chicago's *Black Belt* on the South Side. His family lived comfortably and he never knew

A Case of Rape

want. He attended Wendell Phillips high school, which was then Chicago's all-Negro high school, and starred in basketball and on the track team. He was a brilliant student and could have obtained one of the many scholarships to Chicago University. But instead he chose to attend New York University to escape the racial restrictions in Chicago.

He was on the track team of NYU, but did not go out for basketball because it took too much time from his studies. He was a conscientious student and received high grades.

He lived the typical life of a student in New York's Greenwich Village, and had the usual love affairs with white girls and fraternized with white students. During this time he came under the spell of the communists, whose national headquarters on 12th Street was not far from where he lived. Despite the fact—or perhaps because of it—that the communist party had fallen into ill repute, he became a member.

During his second year he was drafted into the army and served eighteen months. While he was at camp his mother received a legacy of $10,000. at the death of a rich white cotton exporter in New Orleans who was assumed to be her father, although no one said as much.

Ted was furious at what he termed the insolence

of the bequest. He hated the white man who might have been his grandfather. He felt shamed by the implication of his mother's illegitimacy. Nevertheless, he accepted money from his mother to go to Paris and enroll in the Sorbonne. She provided him with an income of fifty dollars weekly.

He was studying political science in view of seeking his career among the newly emerging African states.

At the time of the trial he had been in Paris for one year and had just prepared to begin his second year at the Sorbonne. He spoke French excellently, and had gained a reputation among the leftist international writer-artist-refugee set, which made the *Café Tournon* its headquarters, as being extremely brilliant and an astute political analyst. This was attributable more to his manner than to his sagacity.

He was always intense, given to a petulant impatience with the discourse of others. He had become a member of the French communist party, connected with the super-intellectual cell that held shop on rue Pierre Curie, that section of the Fifth arrondissement flanked by such landmarks in the progress of civilization as the Sorbonne, the Lycée Louis le Grand, Ecole Droit, the Panthéon, the Institut Oceanographique, L'Hôpital Curie, to mention a few. This qualified him as an indisputable authority on the world situation.

A Case of Rape

He found plenty of time for women, yet he liked, even sexually, only the most intelligent of women.

That summer, on vacation to the English Isle of Wight, off the port of Southampton in the Channel, he had become tentatively engaged to a New England American white woman, six years his senior, who was a professor of English literature at a woman's college in Vermont. Her name was Pamela Dickinson Furness, Edmund Furness being the name of her former husband, a professor at a men's university. She had three children, two sons aged nine and five, and a daughter of eight, who had been given to her care by the terms of her divorce.

She was ending a year's Sabbatical spent in England studying its literature at the source when Ted met her. Technically, Ted was vacationing with an English woman whose husband was vacationing in Paris. He and Pamela had fallen in love at once. She had decided to give up her job with the college in Vermont and move her family to Paris, where she and Ted would establish residence after their marriage in December.

Before this transpired, Ted had been arrested and convicted of murdering and raping another American white woman, ten years her senior.

A Case of Rape

SCOTT HAMILTON

Scott Hamilton was the oldest of the defendants and the only one who did not like Paris. He had never found anywhere that he liked, and now he never would.

Scott was a born dreamer. He was forty-six years old at the time of the trial, and he was still a dreamer. None of his dreams had ever come true. But to Scott this was not the most important thing. The most important thing was to dream.

What Scott disliked most about Paris was what it did to the dreamers who gravitated there. It was not the manner in which it destroyed the young and foolish dreams placed hourly on its altar. It was the manner of destroying the capacity for dreaming. All meanings were changed and distorted, or perhaps they were given their true definition and shape, which was equally destructive. Love became sexuality; aspirations became ambition. Achievement was limited to a single day, culminating in bed, yours or someone else's, where everything Parisian was reputedly made. One traded in a dream of happiness for a night of love.

Roger Garrison never discovered that Scott was a

A Case of Rape

dreamer, although he and Scott had been friends off and on for fifteen years. Once when discussing Scott with Shelly Russell, Roger said Scott was too old to have come to Paris. People of his age, with his background, found it hard, if not impossible, to adjust to Paris. Paris was too much like themselves, tired, jaded, blasé and cynical. People were always intolerant of their own vices when seen in another.

That much was indisputable. In the three and one half years Scott had been moving about Europe, a year of which had been spent in France, he had not even learned the rudiments of the French language. And he was not stupid; he had a master's degree in philosophy. He merely had an antagonism toward the city.

Scott didn't look like a dreamer should look. He had the appearance of career soldiers of the British Empire who have spent their lifetimes with dysentery, yellow jaundice and mental blankness in the outposts of East India, or of those raceless octoroons suffering in exile and poverty on yellow-dust farms in eastern Mississippi, denied by both blacks and whites. He was tall, thin, and looked dried out, with cadaverous Anglo-Saxon features, a blank look and a clay-colored complexion. In Europe, only his kinky hair, of a rusty shade and thin on top, identified his Negro ancestry.

A Case of Rape

Unless he kept a careful control over his features, or else kept them propped in the contours of a set, indulgent smile, he always appeared on the verge of exhaustion, with the right side of his mouth sagging in a horrible grimace. He was so quickly bored in most gatherings, he chilled people unconsciously by this grim, exhausted look.

Yet for all of that, most people thought he looked distinguished. He dressed conservatively in impeccable taste. Among persons of almost any race or nationality, he looked different, as though he didn't belong anywhere. This gave the impression that he might be interesting and exciting.

It could not be said that Scott was from any city. In his passport, New York City was listed as birthplace by an error which he didn't take the trouble to correct, and "publicist" as his profession.

As a matter of fact, he was born in Charleston, South Carolina, the youngest of five children and the only son of a Presbyterian minister. When he was four, his family moved to Denver, Colorado, where he grew up in the Negro district around "Five Points," graduated from the Negro high school, and attended the University of Denver with white students for six years to get his master's degree. He majored in philosophy because he didn't want to be a

A Case of Rape

minister, or anything else, and that was the easiest way to circumvent his father, who had always had a profound admiration for the ancient Greek philosophers.

They lived in a large, pleasant brick rectory, which was entirely surrounded by an immense garden of obliterated flowerbeds, neglected fruit trees, rotting wooden benches, broken stone statues, and an excellent, well-kept hammock where his father meditated.

Scott was spoiled by his sisters, his mother, the members of his father's congregation, the gamblers and hustlers and sporting-class people of Five Points, and the white people of Denver who were intrigued by such a white-looking little colored boy with such strange "nigger hair."

His kinky hair came from his mother. She was a Negro woman of the type known among other Negroes as a "high yellow woman with bad hair." His father's hair was light brown and straight. In fact, his father looked like a white person except for his dark brown maroon-tinted eyes. He was a tall, thin man affecting a beard that gave him a startling resemblance to Abraham Lincoln.

Reverend Hamilton's mother, whose maiden name was Sarah Fairfax, began writing a biographical account of the colored branches of the Hamilton and Fairfax families in her declining years. According to

A Case of Rape

her document, derived chiefly from hearsay, her son, Reverend Hamilton, was a direct descendant of the famous American statesman, Alexander Hamilton, and various octoroons with some of the best blood of England mixed with piddling drops from kingly African chiefs. As for herself, alone, she was the absolute daughter of the great southern gentleman, Civil War hero, plantation and slave owner, Major James George Fairfax, of the South Carolina Fairfaxes, whose ancestry went in a straight line of descent back to Baron Thomas Fairfax III, the great English parliamentary general of the 17th century. While it was true that her mother had been a slave, yet she had been the daughter of Major Fairfax's Irish overseer and a beautiful Indian girl. And though she, Sarah Fairfax, herself, had been born a slave, since her mother, although the daughter of an overseer, had been a slave, nevertheless her father, Major Fairfax, had permitted all five of her brothers and sisters to bear his name. Practically all of the white Fairfaxes in South Carolina, that is, those to the manor born, were her blood relatives, but of course she wouldn't tell anybody this outside of the family.

Making allowances for the perfectly natural romanticizing about the bloodlines of the slave women who bore their masters' children, and perhaps the

A Case of Rape

introduction of Alexander Hamilton as an ancestor, her facts were accurate.

Reverend Hamilton's wife, Scott's mother, made no such claim to distinguished forebears. She had her white blood and plenty of it, for everyone to see, no matter where it came from.

Yet, instead of being proud of his white ancestry, Scott was always vaguely ashamed of it. It had come by way of illegitimacy, no matter how distinguished it might be, as though he were equally descended from a line of whores as from lords. And in particular, he had always despised his hair. If his hair could not have been straight to go with his fair complexion, he would rather his complexion have been black to go with his kinky hair.

As a consequence of this vague shame, when he finished college he gravitated toward the sporting class people, who were shameless; and unbeknownst to his parents became a pickup man for the numbers racket operating in the colored section. His parents thought that he was selling insurance for a Negro insurance company.

Scott made money, wore expensive clothes, bought a car, and indulged in the night life about Five Points. He met a seventeen year old girl named Stella Browning singing in one of the joints. She was a full-bodied,

A Case of Rape

café au lait, black haired piece of red hot sex, rotten to the core. She had served a year in the women's reformatory for deserting an illegitimate baby she'd had when she was fifteen; and she was then, in addition to singing, working as an amateur whore and sleeping free with three men, two colored and one white. But she had a voice.

That had been in 1936, when Scott was twenty-six years old, twenty years previous to his conviction. He had married her, perhaps because she was a challenge, perhaps as revenge against his white ancestors.

He became her manager, husband, lover and pimp, taking her from city to city throughout the nation. He taught her manners, how to dress, how to "act a lady if you can't be one," and made her learn to sing. He pushed her career until it got too big for him, then he turned her over to the biggest theatrical agency of that time, and gave them one-third of her earnings.

Scott missed serving in the war by keeping one jump ahead of the age level and working as an "impresario" for the USO. He was married to the talent and he made Stella sing on every occasion.

By the end of the war Stella was a famous big-name singer known throughout the world. Between her recordings and nightclub engagements and motion picture work she was grossing more than one hundred and fifty thousand dollars a year. Taxes, agent's fee and expenses cut it down to fifty thousand, but still they were rich.

Scott tried to introduce her into Negro high society. His father's and grandmother's relatives, the colored branches of the Hamilton and Fairfax families, were socially prominent all up and down the east coast, from Boston to Charleston. But Stella soon learned that his family was no asset to her career, and she refused to accept their domineering condescensions. In her defiance she treated them naturally, as though they had all come out of the same gutter.

Scott grew ashamed of her and they separated. Neither wanted a divorce for reasons of expediency. She put Scott on an allowance of five thousand dollars a year, and he became a remittance man.

Tired and disgusted with life, he left the United States for his first trip to Europe in 1953.

He met Mrs. Hancock on shipboard.

She was everything his wife was not. She was white, intelligent, descendant of a passenger of the Mayflower, a Smith College graduate, of assured social position anywhere in the United States, a native Bostonian.

She was unsuccessful in the only thing she had ever tried to do on her own, her marriage.

A Case of Rape

She was unhappy, lonely, lost.

She had children from whom she was separated.

She wanted to begin a career as a writer.

He fell in love with her.

And she fell desperately in love with him. Later she told him, "When I first looked into your eyes, I knew you were the one person in the world for me."

One month after they reached France, she left her husband to get a divorce and returned to live with Scott in Paris.

Scott took her to a small town in the south of France so she could relax. He called her his Lisbeth.

While they were there, Stella arrived for an engagement in Paris. When she learned that Scott had gone off to the *Cote d'Azur* with a white woman, she sent for him to come to Paris and spend two weeks with her. He didn't answer her.

Two months later he took Lisbeth to London to work on her book. When she began to suffer from the London cold and fog, he took her to Mallorca.

Stella stopped his remittance. After six months in Mallorca they were without money or income. Lisbeth offered to ask her husband for money, but Scott opposed. She did not want to ask her relatives.

Scott wrote to his Negro wife for money to continue to live with his white mistress. She sent enough

A Case of Rape

for their fares back to Paris. Then she met Scott and offered him five thousand dollars in cash and Elizabeth's fare back to America if he would get rid of her. Lisbeth persuaded him to accept it. She would go back to Boston and try to sell the book she had written. If that proved successful she would return to him. By then she would have her divorce and he should also try to get his divorce. They would outwit Stella.

When she went home, Scott went to London. But after two months he couldn't bear being away from her any longer, and returned to New York.

But they could not live together, for she lived with her relations in Boston and he lived in a hotel in New York. They spent the remainder of his five thousand dollars commuting between New York and Boston.

When Stella discovered they were continuing their affair, she again stopped his monthly remittance. Lisbeth returned to Europe in July to spend the summer vacation with her children, but Scott did not get enough money to follow her until December.

Details of the end of the affair had been presented at the trial. How they had tried to live together again; and how they had finally separated. The letter to the publisher concerning his participation in her book. Their rendezvous at the *Café Monaco*. Her death.

9. Roger's Findings

Roger had discovered nothing that was not already known or assumed. He unearthed no startling revelations, came across no new data, found no new clues.

There was nothing to refute the implication that the four Negro defendants were inferior persons despite the fact, that in all likelihood, they might be considered superior Negroes. He had facts to show there were no great differences of character, upbringing, education, intelligence and morals between them and a sampling of white men of any nationality. But he knew such facts were not believable. In order to convince the white race that these four Negroes were not inferior persons, he would have to present irrefutable evidence that they were superior persons, superior in the right sense. And this he could not do.

He had amassed no convincing evidence that they were types who were unlikely to have committed rape. Furthermore, what kind of evidence would this be? With such evidence as he had gathered, he could only convince those who desired to be convinced.

This shocked and infuriated Roger particularly.

64

A Case of Rape

With the exception of Caesar Gee, all were Negroes who revered cultured American white women; desired them perhaps, in a dreamlike manner, as wives, but would always hold them sexually inviolable. Instead of establishing the unlikelihood of their committing this rape, he had merely, to himself at least, proven their innocence and convinced himself that the doctors had lied about the victim being sexually used, which he considered not only conceivable but, under the circumstances, natural. He had hoped secretly he might discover them to be guilty, but yet of such irrefutable culture as to make this appear convincingly unlikely, such as the impression given by career Englishmen in colonial posts of finding black women not only undesirable but abhorrent, yet being unable to account for the mulatto children in their vicinity. Furthermore, Roger Garrison loved violence when committed upon the white race, and regretted such was not the case.

He had found nothing to support his premise that all such convictions of Negro men for raping white women were political manifestations of international racism to keep the black race in subjugation. That this was so, he felt to be indisputable. He also believed that France was initiating the United States' brand of racism as a political maneuver, somewhat

A Case of Rape

in the manner of Gallic Uncle Toming, to gain the backing and support of the United States in the Suez Canal crisis and their Algerian war. But he had found no evidence to spotlight this in world opinion, to remove the doubt, to make such truth impregnable. After all, people who were cognizant of the political aspects of racism knew this to be true. But he found nothing to convince the masses.

What proved the most disappointing was his failure to establish a convincing relationship between this conviction and his own political usage, thereby proving he had been cast in the role of a literary failure to serve political racism.

The world was already convinced that the four defendants were superior Negroes. In fact, all but one of them possessed what was considered the superior blood of the white race. Yet the world was convinced they had committed this crime of raping a white woman. What then could be expected from other Negroes, the common herd of blacks, who were not even blessed with the enlightening blood of whites?

Should he try to draw a parallel with himself to support his contention, the world would ask: What makes Roger Garrison any different from these other superior Negroes?

In the end he had to confess his investigation had failed.

10. Roger's Errors

It is to be noted that Roger made a number of appalling errors in both outlook and execution of his investigation.

First was his assumption that white Frenchmen would consider him in any other light than as a political gimmick.

Second was that there were any great numbers of people who had ever doubted the unlikelihood of these four particular Negroes raping this particular white woman. In fact, only the very ignorant had ever really believed it.

Third was that there were any great numbers of intelligent people who were not already thoroughly convinced that the wholesale convictions of Negro men for raping white women were evidence of political racism.

In addition, Roger did not thoroughly investigate

A Case of Rape

the relationship existing between the defendants. He committed the customary error of white persons who assume that Negroes love one another. Strangely enough, it never occurred to Roger that one or more of the defendants might have been lying; that there might have existed between them a bitter hatred.

He showed a startling lack of concern for the facts of what had actually happened in the room where Mrs. Hancock had died. Had Mrs. Hancock taken the aphrodisiac accidentally, as the defense had contended; or from coercion, as the prosecution had contended? Or had she taken it deliberately, a possibility which somehow had been overlooked. Had she taken it to stimulate her sexual desire? Had she taken it to kill herself?

His major error consisted of his indifference to the fact of the defendants' guilt or innocence, on the premise that it did not matter.

Roger was so accustomed to condemning the dominant white group for the crimes committed by the oppressed black minorities, he completely ignored the fundamental principle in the moral fabric of a democratic society, the assumption of innocence.

Had he assumed the defendants' innocence from the start, he might have realized at once that the most important question posed by the trial, the one most

A Case of Rape

damning to the doctrine of white supremacy, remained unanswered to the end.

It was not the question of whether Mrs. Hancock had been raped and murdered.

It was the question of why she was there, in that
hotel room, alone with four Negro men, if she could
believe that Negro men were potential rapists?

Why was she there? That was the question for the
racists to answer.

He would have been electrified by the discovery
that this is the one question the dominant white society never explores in convictions of Negro men
for raping white women; never has and never will.

Roger knew, of course, the bitter joke told among
American Negroes in the Latin Quarter: That the
surest way of coercing an American white woman
into sleeping with them, especially if she was from the
South, was to charge her with being prejudiced, and
say scornfully to her that she is afraid some of the
black will rub off onto her, or ask her when was the
last time she had a nigger lynched.

But it did not occur to him to relate this evil story
to the possibility that the desperate struggle by the
white race to maintain supremacy might very likely
be making the white female more and more vulnerable
to rape. That to maintain white domination by the

A Case of Rape

means of persecuting Negroes might render the white woman as defenseless against persecution by Negroes as Negroes themselves against persecution by white men.

He might then have arrived at an outlook where it appeared perfectly conceivable that before the end of this long, slow, torturous, losing struggle by the white race to continue its racial domination, the white woman might, to a great degree, and of an absolute necessity, become expendable.

This indifference to the guilt or innocence of the defendants accounted for the fact that Roger made no thorough investigation into the life of Mrs. Hancock and her love affair with Scott Hamilton. He had assumed from his brutal attitude toward such cases that Mrs. Hancock was like all other American white women lusting after Negro men. That she, like the others, had come to Paris to be loved by them. That she had deserted her husband and children for the sole purpose of sharing Scott Hamilton's bed.

Roger had met Mrs. Hancock shortly after she had first joined Scott in Paris in 1953. Scott had taken her to visit Roger. She had never heard of Roger and her first impression of him had been dreadful.

Roger always felt inferior and ill at ease in the presence of American white women of Mrs. Hancock's heritage. He was aware of this, and it infuriated him, but he could not help it. He felt as though he wore in his manner his poor, oppressed upbringing in Alabama, as they did in theirs the results of their upbringings in the ultimate of American culture.

In addition to which she was so obviously superior in outward aspect to his lower class French wife, the comparison seemed personally insulting.

As a consequence he had been inexcusably rude and uncouth. But when he observed that Mrs. Hancock assumed this to be his true character, he never forgave her.

Therefore it was painful and humiliating for Roger to think of Mrs. Hancock objectively. So he had ignored her in his investigation.

Had he not done so, he certainly would have asked himself the question: *Why was she there?* One can not be raped if one is absent.

He might have wondered how the French would have answered the question about a French woman. What explanation could they offer to lend aid and obeisance to the doctrine of white supremacy that would be any more convincing than Americans'? Or what could the Swedes offer that would be any more valid than the Germans'?

There are many people in this world who know

the answer. White people and black people. People of all races.

But of the five persons connected with the case, only two of them knew exactly. Scott and Mrs. Hancock.

11. Mrs. Hancock

Mrs. Hancock was a casualty of white Christian society which fails to enforce the moral laws it has ordained. She was one of those unfortunate victims of a code of ethics promulgated by the white race as its own private doctrine for the elevation of whites only; a code of ethics which the white race has been the only race to reject.

In a society where man's inhumanity to man has attained recognition as normal behavior, where the inflicting of mental and emotional hurts, not only needlessly, but senselessly, has become a universal pastime, she believed this to be sinful. Her aunt, who had raised her, had taught her in childhood that needless injury inflicted on another was the greatest sin of all. Mrs. Hancock still believed this at her death.

A Case of Rape

Mrs. Hancock was at heart a puritan. She had been reared meticulously in puritanism. A fortune had been spent on giving her a puritanical education. She had been taught to believe in God and in goodness, no matter how wicked you might wish to be. For her the Bible was a source of both solace and joy. But she had not been taught that in her white Christian culture these beliefs were objects of ridicule.

On her father's side she was descended from the John Hancock who had signed the *Declaration of Independence.*

Her mother could have traced her ancestry to a militant Huguenot who had fled France to England in the 16th century, and whose eldest son had been one of the 102 separatists from the Church of England, immortalized in history as the Pilgrim Fathers, who had landed from the *Mayflower* at Plymouth Rock on American soil in 1620.

Her father, Lawrence Everett Hancock, had been a counsellor-at-law connected with a Boston law firm of great prominence. He had been active in Boston civic and cultural affairs, but like many members of old American families, had had little wealth.

Elizabeth, born in 1916, was the youngest of three children. Her brother, Geoffrey Glen, was the oldest, and Margaret next.

A Case of Rape

During the first world war her father went with the AEF to Europe as a colonel and was killed in July of 1918 in the battle of the *Marne*.

Her mother died two years later.

The three children were taken by a poor aunt, who remained a spinster and dedicated her life to their upbringing.

They lived in a pleasant house on a shady hill in Back Bay, Boston, overlooking the Charles River. From their well-kept backyard they could see the ivy-covered buildings of Harvard University across the river, and on bright days watch the Harvard crews working their sculls.

When Elizabeth was ten, the three children were left a legacy of $150,000, to be divided equally among them upon reaching the age of twenty-one. Their benefactor was a grand aunt on their father's side who left the bulk of her seven million dollar fortune to Smith College and Harvard University.

The son attended Harvard and the two daughters Smith.

Geoffrey died of pneumonia in his senior year.

In 1934, Elizabeth and Margaret went to Paris and entered the Sorbonne as exchange students.

They were both small, dark blonde and quite pretty, and appallingly ignorant of the most rudi-

A Case of Rape

mentary knowledge relating to sex. They had learned dancing and horseback riding and swimming and good manners beneficial to the process of living. And they had been drilled in such facts as where babies come from, and why. But neither of them could define the exact difference between an orgasm and an organism, nor did they understand exactly what a boy wanted with them after they had danced with him.

At first they were assumed to be lesbians masquerading as sisters. But when it was discovered they were truly sisters and in reality virgins, all was forgiven.

After the knowledge of their virginity became publicized, they were wooed with an intensity that was frightening.

Margaret escaped; she fled back to the United States and married a Harvard-educated proper Bostonian medical doctor.

But Elizabeth was overwhelmed and married by a young Belgian student enrolled in the College of Dentistry, André Brissaud. She had been unprepared for his campaign which ran the gamut of emotions, from jealous rages to tearful contrition; and she had been still more unprepared for marriage.

André Brissaud was that type of European whose profession is sex and whose occupation, whatever it might be, but an avocation. He was imbued with an ingrown, refined evil of generations of decadence; an evil distilled from all the dark superstitions of countless centuries of Christian expedience and aged in the slowly rotting *bien faite* culture of a blasé and jaded city. His was an ungodly evil that was all the more terrible because he didn't know it was evil. An evil that had been in existence for so long it had attained another status, termed by the Americans as *continental*. He would have been amazed, affronted, deeply insulted, had someone called him evil.

As a consequence he brought to their marriage a lust which she found shattering. He could not have her without surgery, so he had such necessary surgery performed by three friends, young internes in the College of Surgery, and had her immediately afterwards. He truly thought she would enjoy the pain.

He felt her to be a possession, and he was never any more tender toward her than toward any of his other possessions, his dog or his car.

When she became pregnant for the first time, André persuaded her to claim her legacy. The money was divided equally between her and Margaret, and with the $75,000, which was her share, André bought a dental practice in the French-speaking city of Dinant, Belgium, on the Meuse River.

A Case of Rape

Elizabeth bore him three daughters before the war. She was caught by the German invasion and remained in Dinant for the duration of the war. Because of her excellent command of the French language and her student identifications from Paris, the German occupation authorities assumed her to be French, and she escaped being interned. Or perhaps they chose to overlook her because André collaborated with the Wehrmacht in the capacity of civilian dentist. Anyway, Elizabeth was in no position to object and they suffered few hardships.

A fourth daughter was born during the war.

Following the German surrender, André was sentenced to a year in military prison because of his Nazi activities. Elizabeth remained in Dinant with her four daughters until his release, out of a sense of loyalty commensurate with her other puritanical qualities; and then, foolishly, attempted to escape with her daughters to America.

Following a wild all-night automobile flight, pursued by André and four friends, she managed to cross the border into Holland with her three oldest daughters, but had to leave the baby with its nurse behind.

She took her three daughters to live with her aunt in Boston and filed suit against André for divorce.

She was granted an American divorce with custody

A Case of Rape

of her children, but it was not recognized in Belgium and her husband refused to give up their baby.

A year later she returned to her husband for the sake of her baby and tried to repair their marriage.

She became pregnant again and gave birth to a still-born baby. She was suffering from a severe hemorrhage and was not told her baby was dead until she'd gotten from her bed and wandered into the corridor in search of it.

She was permitted to select its burial clothes from the baby clothes she had made for the christening, and later she saw its body in the tiny casket.

The day after its burial, an attendant nurse, by mistake, brought her another baby at feeding time. She became convinced the living baby was hers and the nurses had made a mistake attributing the dead baby to her.

When the baby was taken from her, she went temporarily insane. This was followed by a complete mental breakdown. Her husband attempted to have her put into an insane asylum.

Aided by a United States newspaper correspondent, she again escaped and returned to Boston; but this time leaving all of her children behind.

She spent a year in a mental institution in Massachusetts before recovering.

A Case of Rape

She was returning to see her husband and children in April of 1953 when she met Scott Hamilton on shipboard and fell in love with him.

12. Scott and Elizabeth

The most important thing about this affair was not what happened, or how it happened, but that it could happen.

It was natural for it to happen. These two people were not too far apart in race, upbringing, or religion. They had the same traditions, the same moral outlook, the same disappointments by goodness and God.

The first impression Scott had of Mrs. Hancock was of softness. She had a soft, shy manner to go with her soft, appealing voice; soft brown eyes to go with her soft modest hesitancy. Had she been younger, he would have thought her demure. But she wasn't demure in any sense. She had an absolute passion for life; she loved laughter, dancing, people, animals, things and places. She even loved ships, after eighteen crossings, while Scott hated the sickness he felt on his first.

A Case of Rape

The second was of goodness. She reminded him of a Dostoevski character; her goodness seemed to derive from a lack of appreciation of the pleasures and benefits of evil.

The third was of fear. She was deathly afraid of the strangest things; the long lines of closed cabin doors in an empty corridor; men standing alone in the shadows. He didn't understand this until he learned of her having been confined to a mental institution.

These things made a profound impression on Scott. For fifteen years he had been married to a woman who was neither soft, good nor afraid.

When he told her he was going to Paris in search of peace and quiet she laughed until she became slightly hysterical. By way of explanation, he told her about his wife, the great blues singer, Stella Browning. She understood then. That broke the ice.

Mrs. Hancock talked to him about her husband and marriage with a frankness he found almost unbearable. She told him that in all the years of her marriage, after five pregnancies, she had never had an orgasm with her husband and had not known, until after a brief affair with a friend in Boston, how a woman could possibly enjoy sex. He would not have believed this of any other woman he had ever known.

He gathered that her husband thought her frigid;

A Case of Rape

and that within her there had raged a conflict between her feelings of sexual inferiority and spiritual superiority. She said her husband was extremely handsome; and that he took sex stimulants and went with several different women every week of his life.

Finally he came to the conclusion that it was only her husband whom she feared. She was repulsed by him and degraded by his incessant promiscuousness. Nevertheless, he had the ability to cast a sexual spell over her when she was in his presence. He dominated her against her will, like a snake charming a bird, and forced her to submit to the indignities of his lust.

She was returning to him to see her children. But she did not want to live with him again. Yet she was deathly afraid he would subdue her, and by so doing drive her permanently insane.

He knew her fear was genuine. He never got over it. From the beginning to the end of their affair, he always felt a little sick whenever he really thought of her.

Yet she held a sexual attraction for him greater than he had ever felt for any other woman.

He tried to reassure her, comfort her, stabilize her emotions to withstand her husband's sexual dominance. He explained to her the communistic tactic of defining and re-defining a single stand over and over again, changing the definition but never the principle, as though compromising, modifying, relenting, yet never relinquishing the basic objectives formed at the outset. He convinced her that the main thing was for her to refrain from sleeping with her husband, for whatever reasons it might be necessary to devise.

She was impressed. She told Scott that he was a complete person. She thought of her husband as a complete person also. She wished that she, herself, was a complete person.

Scott never fully understood how this applied. Knowing how incomplete and insecure he really was, her compliment irritated him. And from the picture she'd given of her husband, Scott imagined him to be a homosexual, or, as is often said, bi-sexual. He told her as much. But she did not believe it.

Her husband met her in his car at Le Havre. Scott went to Paris by the boat train.

She had promised to return to him. She wrote him long spiritually passionate letters, as many as two and three daily. She poured out her innermost feelings. He was constantly shocked by those unrestrained revelations of a puritanical woman's soul.

He knew that her letters served to keep his image alive in the sexual contest with her husband. He resented it. He became firmly convinced that she was mentally very sick, on the borderline. His sense of reality told him to reject her while there was still time; to forget her completely or he could kiss his peace of mind goodbye.

Yet, when she telephoned him from Dinant one day, and asked if he still wanted her to come to him, he told her to come and promised her that everything would be all right.

Scott took his Lisbeth first to the village of Le Trayas on the *Cote d'Azur*. They rented a villa overlooking the sea, and reveled in the warm sunshine. She began to relax. Shortly she began work on her book.

Scott was a sensualist of an extreme degree. Yet he abhorred the thought of sensuality in her husband. And the fact that she had been so terribly hurt by the type of sensuality that possessed himself, touched his soul. He never thought of their different races, the fact that she was white and he was colored. It never occurred to him that she was as much a casualty of racism as himself—an inverted sort of racism that perpetuates the dominance of the male. He merely thought of her as sick. And to cure her sick mind, heal her hurt soul, restore both her mind and spirit to normality, became the purpose of his life. There were

A Case of Rape

times when he felt that her rehabilitation was the only reason he had been born.

As a consequence, from first to last, his love for her was but a dream, acting itself out in his mind. And she was only someone he had dreamed into existence. The real Elizabeth Hancock he never saw and never knew.

From France they went to London and lived in a quiet flat in Hamstead near the Heath until January of the next year.

In London they were ignored. They were as remote from their environment as though residing at the North Pole, and yet with all the conveniences of modern life. They found security in their isolation.

But in Mallorca the white world began to intrude again. The American and English exiles living there were curious and would not let them alone.

When their money ran out and Scott had to appeal to his wife, Mrs. Hancock began getting sick again.

She had never looked to Scott for financial security. Her own world could give her that. She could have had security from her husband in a material sense. Why couldn't he understand she didn't need food, she thought; she didn't need clothing, she didn't need shelter.

A Case of Rape

She had abandoned that kind of security sixteen months before when she had left her home and her children and her kind to come to him and lose herself in the soft dark night of his love. To her he was not only escape, but a dark void of peace beyond escape, free from all the anxieties and hurts and demands of her race and culture. A dark void without thought, that had no past or future, no pretensions or necessities. Hidden in his beautiful, impenetrable night from all the despair and indignities of life, where women were the second sex, and the pride in race they fed upon.

But Scott did not understand this until it was too late; and had Roger Garrison understood it, he would have known from the start of his investigation, *why she was there, in that room with four Negro men, where she died.*

As a consequence Scott was tortured by his inability to provide for her, and he resented her lack of sympathy for his dilemma. So they returned to Paris, where they had begun.

By the time they had spent six weeks of misunderstanding and anxiety in a dark Paris hotel room, their love had become a nightmare. Scott accepted the money from his wife and sent his Lisbeth home in an attempt to save what was left of their love.

A Case of Rape

Mrs. Hancock wanted very much to be a brave and honest woman, the same as Scott Hamilton wanted very much to be a brave and honest man. But the burden of racial prejudice in the United States is borne by the white woman and the Negro man. And when Scott finally returned to the United States to find Lisbeth again, she had almost disappeared in the maze of racial barriers.

When Mrs. Hancock had returned to Paris and begun work in the American Hospital, Scott followed her again and tried to rekindle the flame of their romance. But it was over. Both knew it in their hearts, even though for a short time they tried to make it work again.

Her last trip back to Paris alone had made Mrs. Hancock a sensualist. Sensualism became her escape. Like it does to all persons who try to escape in it late in life, it had strange effects on her. She became cowardly and dishonest.

During his last effort to live with her, Scott became sick himself. He contracted all the forms of mental illness he had tried from the beginning to cure in her. He suffered all the fears and frustrations and anxieties and paranoia she had first suffered.

He reached a stage where he could bear it no longer. He was afraid he might kill her. One night in a rage

A Case of Rape

he told her to get out of his room and out of his life. She got up and walked out and stayed away. He permitted her to return for her belongings.

At first Scott could not get her out of his mind. He thought of her constantly.

Once he dreamed that he was taking her some place, but he didn't know where. They were crossing a street. He took her arm, feeling that everything was all right again. He felt very tender toward her, as he had felt in the past. She was wearing a beautiful beige silk dress. Her graying hair had been recently set and she looked very attractive. They came to a cluster of shrubs in a small park. Several men were standing nearby. Suddenly she had to urinate and went behind the shrubs. Afterwards she had said accusingly, "Why didn't you take me somewhere I could go without all those men staring at me." He tried to explain that he had realized her necessity. But he noticed that she was very hurt and he began feeling miserable again. He didn't know what was wrong. She broke away from him and began to run. He ran after her as fast as he could, assailed by a premonition that she might try to hurt herself. She turned down a narrow street into which emptied countless narrower streets. When he turned into the street after her, she had disappeared. Desperately he ran from one narrow street to another, trying to find out which one she had taken. But she was gone.

Scott had almost gotten over her and restored his life to a semblance of normality when she telephoned him and made the rendezvous for that fatal Sunday afternoon.

But he never got over the feeling that a terrible, terrible joke had been played on him.

13. The Missing Evidence

Two very important facts were not established in the trial.

First, when Mrs. Hancock went to keep her rendezvous with Scott Hamilton, she was suffering from such torturous anxieties she was mentally unbalanced.

Second, she was physically exhausted and on the verge of collapse.

To begin with, the letter from her publisher requesting that she verify the warranty in her contract had upset her as much by the knowledge that some unknown person wished her harm, as by the probabil-

A Case of Rape

ity that because of this her book might not be published. She was shattered by the discovery she had such spiteful enemies whom she did not know, and sick with speculation why anyone should hate her so. What had she done to so antagonize anyone on earth?

Had she been able to think with objectivity she might have realized she had antagonized the entire white race by living with a Negro; and she had antagonized certain members of the black race also by living with a Negro, *and being a cultured white woman.* But her sheltered intelligence would never have been able to entertain such conceptions.

She did not once believe her enemy was Scott. She could not believe it was because he was a Negro and she had lived with him. She did not dare believe that a Negro man with whom she had lived would deliberately hurt her so, or even hate her. If this were so, there could be no virtue in being white. And she believed in her race as she believed in her God. Yet she was assailed by an insidious dread that perhaps Negro men did wish her harm. But why? she asked herself. It was all so horribly confusing. And it contradicted one of her deepest convictions.

Furthermore, previous to meeting Scott, she had not slept for more than twenty-four hours.

A Case of Rape

Her husband had been with her in her room from the time she returned at four a.m. until an hour before she arose to dress for her rendezvous.

Mrs. Hancock had spent her vacation, the month of August, with her divorced husband, André Brissaud, and her four daughters in a villa on the island of Capri. She had arranged to have only her daughters with her, but at the last moment her husband had insisted on coming also. He had threatened to keep the children at home if she would not permit him to come with them.

She knew he could do this, despite the fact she had been given custody of the children during their summer vacation. He could always find some excuse that would be acceptable to the Belgian courts. Besides which, he knew of her former affair with Scott. She believed he would use that knowledge against her.

Afterwards, she was pleased with his presence.

He seemed to find her more attractive than ever. He had developed a greater sexual desire for her since he had learned of her affair with an American Negro. He courted her ardently, as though she were a new woman he felt compelled to make. He put himself out to be courteous, gallant and desirable.

Since having lived alone in Paris, and tasted the fruits of its sensualism, Mrs. Hancock found her for-

A Case of Rape

mer husband as attractive as he found her. For the first
time she desired him sexually. It did not occur to her
that part of his ardor might stem from the fact that he
believed her book would earn a lot of money in
America.

Only the intervention of their eldest daughter,
Michelle, kept them apart. Michelle had an abnormal
love for her father, and would not let him touch her
mother. She watched them continuously, and never
left them together unobserved for more than a few
minutes. Whenever she awakened in the night, she
looked into their separate rooms to make sure they
were alone.

The resulting frustration only served to inflame
their desire. They became like lovers trying to outwit
a suspicious wife.

It resulted in his asking her to marry him again. The
idea appealed to her. He was well-off financially and
had their large house in Dinant which was rightfully
half her own. She was weary of working and living
alone. She wanted to be with her children.

When they separated at the end of August, he
promised to come to see her in Paris as soon as possible. Impulsively, she gave him her room key and
told him to wait for her in her room and not come to
the hospital if she was at work when he arrived. On

91

A Case of Rape

her return to Paris she told her patron she had lost her key and took the second one. So much time had elapsed before her death the patron had forgotten the incident by the time of the trial.

André arrived in Paris on a Saturday shortly before midnight. On finding a couple entering the hotel by the street door with their night key just as he had started to ring the night bell, he entered behind them and went up to Mrs. Hancock's room. This was not at all unusual and the couple would scarcely have remembered it had they known of its importance; as it happened they never gave it another thought.

André had been driving for five hours steadily and was relieved to find Elizabeth absent. He undressed and went immediately to bed and was asleep by the time she arrived at four o'clock.

Elizabeth had had time to think over his proposal of marriage and was again assailed by doubts and fears. But he had anticipated this and shortly had overcome them by his passionate declaration of love and solemn promises of undying fidelity. He aroused her desire and shortly had regained his sexual dominance. She agreed to re-marry him should she become pregnant.

He had brought with him a bottle of wine containing a few drops of the same aphrodisiac which later

A Case of Rape

killed her, as was his custom when preparing for a night of love. From time to time he sipped the wine, encouraging her to drink it with him. They performed the sex act five times which was rendered possible only by the stimulant.

At the beginning she hoped passionately to become pregnant again. She wanted to have another baby for the last time.

But the over-indulgence left her feeling humiliated, dirty and debased again. She was at such a low ebb of physical vitality, her mental resistance was shattered. When André left her, she again became beset by all the fears and anxieties she had experienced during her mental illness. She felt so depressed that suicide seemed preferable to returning to the agony of her former marriage. She did not realize that her state of mind derived, in part, from her physical depletion.

As a consequence, when she went to meet Scott Hamilton, she was very much in need of reassurance on all counts. She needed his love and kindness to regain her self-esteem and sense of personal honor and dignity. She felt certain that Scott still respected her. She believed too, despite everything, that he still loved her. Her husband had aroused her passion and greedily consumed her body. From Scott she wanted only tenderness.

A Case of Rape

In her book she had written: "Women are so silly. They are so vulnerable to tenderness."

Scott would be tender towards her. In her desperate need, she convinced herself that all Negro men were tender towards white women.

Scott was also upset and suffering from his own sense of guilt. When she had telephoned him, and told him what had happened, he had known at once that Roger Garrison was the person who had written to her publisher. Roger was the only person Scott had told of his interest in Mrs. Hancock's book.

But even without this fact, Scott would have known it was Roger who had done it. It was the kind of knowledge that Negroes have of one another; which most white people will never understand. Scott knew that Roger was secretly envious of his worldliness, of his imagined successes with cultured white women and his imagined life of adventure without responsibilities. Roger had come from the poorest of backgrounds and had achieved fame and success by dint of an unusual talent and conscientious application; and he resented other Negroes whom he assumed enjoyed life's benefits without struggle. He knew that Roger considered him more or less a type of pimp.

And he knew that Roger had always been envious of his affair with Mrs. Hancock because of her hered-

A Case of Rape

ity. Roger would have liked for him to have acted the part of a pimp; he felt that Scott was debasing his Negro wife, Stella Browning, by his courteous attitude toward Mrs. Hancock, and the love and respect he had given her.

In addition, he knew that Roger hated Mrs. Hancock because he felt she looked upon him condescendingly. Roger could have combatted her hatred, even have welcomed it; but her contempt unmanned him.

It had never occurred to Roger that Mrs. Hancock rarely thought of him at all, and then only with pity.

When she and Scott had separated, Roger had wanted Scott to seek revenge. He had tried in all manner of devious ways to provoke Scott into hurting and humiliating her by starting some vicious rumor that might undermine her job in the American Hospital and her position with other white Americans in Paris.

This Scott had refused to do. As a consequence, Roger hated Mrs. Hancock all the more.

It was for this reason more than any other that Scott had taken her to visit his friends on that fatal afternoon.

She had confessed to him that she had been with her

A Case of Rape

husband since four o'clock that morning and how it had left her feeling. It humiliated him to be her confessor, but he had tried to assure her that it might work out for the best. If she became pregnant again her baby would occupy her life. She would have her children again. Perhaps she would find that to be enough, no matter what her husband did. She was a mother and should be with her children. She should not worry too much about the European sex habits of her husband.

He tried in all the ways he knew to comfort her and calm her fears. But he did not really care anymore. He discovered during those few moments they were together in the *Café Monaco* that he was completely over her.

It was only to reaffirm her faith in Negro men that he took her to his room to meet his three friends. He did not know why that seemed to be so important at the time. It was as if, in some manner, he felt that he must defend the dignity and integrity of his race. And he knew that his friends would give her all the flattery and attention and respect intelligent and cultured Negro men always bestow on upperclass white women.

At that time Shelly Russell was having an affair with a white American divorcee with two children

A Case of Rape

and Theodore Elkins was engaged to another cultured white American woman.

The fact that two of Scott's friends had such a love and respect for white women of her class inspired Mrs. Hancock with faith and self-confidence. She felt grateful to them for recognizing the high spiritual qualities in women with children who had refused to submit to their husbands' abuses. She respected their sensitivity and was touched by their tenderness and compassion. Their warmth of emotion and gentleness made her feel infinitely safe with them.

She had no qualms whatsoever about lying on Scott's bed and taking a short nap when she became slightly tipsy. She felt that they all liked her and considered her a friend, and she had begun thinking of them as friends also.

It did not occur to her that she had offended Ted Elkins to the quick of his sensitive ego by giving too much attention to Scott and Shelly, and neglecting the conversational offerings of himself and Caesar Gee. Ted attributed this to the fact that he and Caesar Gee looked the most negroid, and construed from this that she was basically a racist.

Of course, Ted did not know that in her state of mind she could scarcely cope with his political brilliance. But he knew that she was an intelligent and cultured woman. He had heard this from many reliable sources. Therefore, to him the only conceivable reason she would ignore him would be because she was anti-Negro.

The simple facts were that she knew Scott—she had been his mistress—and Shelley was an extremely interesting conversationalist and humorist and made her laugh. She wanted so much to laugh.

All of them knew of the bottle of sherry containing Spanish Fly which Scott kept in his room. They knew it had been given to him by a white American journalist, and they knew what the journalist had said on giving it to him. They knew he was experimenting to find the right proportions safe enough to drink. They knew he then intended to give a big racially mixed party and sit back and see what would happen.

It was just pure, spontaneous, unpremeditated, racially-inspired *spite* that provoked Ted into giving the bottle to Mrs. Hancock when she awakened and looked about for the bottle from which she had previously drunk. Ted had no intention whatsoever in harming her seriously. He did not know the dreadful effects of an over-dose of cantharides. He merely intended to maneuver her in the proximity of Caesar Gee when the stimulant began to work. He imagined

A Case of Rape

that she thought of Caesar Gee as an ape; as he had overheard American white women refer to certain Negro men in the *Café Tournon*. He wanted to see how she would respond to an ape in a state of sexual excitement.

Of course Ted knew that Scott would prevent him doing this if he noticed it. In fact, he suspected that Scott might object violently to any action that would humiliate Mrs. Hancock. So he waited until Scott had his back turned when opening the window before passing Mrs. Hancock the bottle.

Caesar Gee did not notice the action at all.

But Shelly Russell did. However, Ted knew Shelly well enough to know he would do nothing to prevent it. Deep inside of Shelly's reverence for this type of white woman, there was an animosity as deep as Ted's own. But Shelly did not know the stimulant could prove fatal either. He merely exchanged glances with Ted and watched Mrs. Hancock clinically with a somewhat brighter twinkle in his eyes as she served herself a drink.

Mrs. Hancock was thinking of that memorable statement in the novel, *The Bridge of San Luis Rey*, spoken by the Abbess, Madre Maria del Pilar, in her astonishment in discovering the humility that had lain hidden in the proud, selfish heart of the Marquessa-de

Montemayor, "Now learn, learn at last that anywhere you may expect grace."

All of the defendants had worked desperately to save her life. All had prayed silently for her to live. Panic had kept them from sending for a doctor. But it would not have saved her anyway. She was too exhausted, physically, emotionally and spiritually, to make the effort to live; she only wanted to jump from the window to her death. Even in the great agony of her death she did not want to return to such a life as she had lived.

14. The Strange Fruits of Fear

It was fear which influenced the four defendants to withhold the evidence that Ted Elkins had given Mrs. Hancock the fatal drink; pure, unadulterated fear. No sense of loyalty to Ted or racial allegiance entered into it. They were simply afraid that no one outside of the American Negro race would believe Ted's motive, that he had done it out of spite.

A Case of Rape

If they had believed that they could have convinced a court composed of white people, anywhere in the world, of Ted's individual guilt, the three others would have testified against him.

But they had been so conditioned by their culture, by the preconceptions and generalizations of the white race which always attributes the crimes of one Negro to the entire Negro race, they could not conceive of a white jury believing their innocence.

If they testified that Ted had given her the bottle deliberately, it would be tantamount to confessing they were all accomplices. And that would have been tantamount to confessing they had given her the aphrodisiac for the purpose of raping her. No one would believe they had not actually raped her.

However, if they contended that she had drunk the potion accidentally, of her own accord, it might not be believed, but at least it would not so easily be refuted.

In their opinion, it was always best for any Negro to deny any charge lodged against him, to deny it totally and continuously, rather than try to explain the degree of his guilt.

The strange thing was that Roger Garrison did not foresee this possibility immediately, even instinctively, as he would have done before coming to live in France.

A Case of Rape

It should have occurred to him at once that American Negroes have been so conditioned by the injustices of American courts that they will automatically plead innocent even in the fact of obvious guilt. There is the bitter joke of the slave caught red-handed with the stolen chicken. His master asks: "Why did you steal that chicken, Rastus?" The slave looks at him with an expression of pure innocence and replies: "What chicken, massah?"

It was also fear that caused Scott Hamilton to withhold the evidence that Mrs. Hancock had been visited that fatal morning by her husband. The fear that he would not be believed and would not be able to prove it.

Scott could not face the chagrin and humiliation which would be his reward for admitting that Mrs. Hancock, his former mistress, had informed him of having been exhausted by the love-making of her former husband a few hours previous to their rendezvous. People would wonder what role he played. Was he her father confessor? Was he a homosexual who could share her ecstasies vicariously. And what in heaven's name would inspire him to impose her upon his friends, to treat her with respect, even reverence, after that?

Scott could not publicly confess, whatever the cost,

A Case of Rape

that after Mrs. Hancock had informed him of her husband's visit, it still had been important to himself to defend the dignity and integrity of his race to her. Had he been nailed to a cross, he could not have confessed to the world that her good opinion meant so much merely because she was white, American, and upperclass. That this was so merely because he, Scott, was himself half-white, half-American, and half-upperclass.

Roger Garrison saw no reason whatsoever to confess that he had written to Mrs. Hancock's publisher. He justified his reasoning by convincing himself that it had no real bearing on the case.

Scott refrained from mentioning it because he did not want to involve Roger in any aspects of the trial and by so doing malign the character of still another Negro; and furthermore he did not feel that it mattered one way or another who wrote the letter.

It is understandable why André Brissaud did not come forward voluntarily with his testimony. The defendants were black and he was white and how could he possibly be a defense witness for black men accused of raping and murdering a white woman, and his former wife at that. What would his race think of him, a white man who, by his own admission, had still desired the body of his former wife after she had once left him to live with a Negro—a Negro later accused of raping and murdering her. He and his daughters were already intolerably ashamed of the fact that Mrs. Hancock had been his former wife and their mother. Was there a single white person on earth who would condemn his attitude?

15. Speculation

If Roger Garrison had unearthed the missing evidence and presented it to the proper authorities, and had then been unsuccessful in gaining a re-trial, he might then have been able to present substantial evidence to support his premise that all convictions of Negro men for raping white women are a part of an international conspiracy to maintain white supremacy.

But since this was not done, one may only speculate.

Would this new evidence have been accepted as valid in a new trial? Would it have been sufficient to convince a court of white men of the innocence of the four Negro defendants. Would it have convinced the people of the world, of all races, of the unlikelihood of these four Negro men of committing the crime of raping a white woman, or any woman of any race?

A Case of Rape

Or would the verdict have been the same and the opinions of people remained unchanged?

Whatever would have been the outcome, one assumption may be drawn. The consciences of men would have had to entertain the charitable element of doubt. No one would again be able to point an accusing finger at all Negro men and think: *They are potential rapists.* Men would have then been influenced to consider whether the greater crime was rape or the conviction of innocent men for rape on racial preconceptions.

Perhaps this might have forwarded the precept of all men of whatever race to bear some measure of the guilt for mankind's greatest crime, man's inhumanity to man.

And that is how it should be. We are all guilty.

Chester Himes
Paris

Postscript

by Calvin Hernton

Chester Himes was born and reared in the United States. But since the early 1950s, he has traveled and lived outside of his native land, in Scandinavia, London, and Paris. He eventually established permanent residence in Spain. Although Himes has lived outside the United States for over thirty years, one of the remarkable things about his writing is that virtually everything he writes concerning black people in America still retains an accuracy that is downright uncanny. It is as though he never left. Since he was first published during the early 1930s, Chester Himes has been a prolific writer of short stories, articles and poems, some twenty-odd novels and two volumes of autobiography. Several of his novels have made the bestseller lists in foreign countries as well as in America. Nothing short of the realism and extraordinary brilliance of his writing can account for Himes's appeal.

A Case of Rape

Yet, today the name and works of Chester Himes are known and appreciated in the United States by only a handful of black literature enthusiasts, close friends, and fellow writers. As is true with all but a few black writers, Chester Himes is not to be found in standard white anthologies, literature texts, or books of criticism.

Because Himes writes in a framework of *social reality* in which characters and incidents are easily recognizable in everyday American life, reviewers, publicity people, and publishers as well have reacted in very mean and unethical ways, even when the books are initially well received by the reading public. More often than not, dirty deals have constituted his lot from the publishing world. He has been consistently robbed of revenues, everybody seemed to have gotten the money but him.

Strange and hurtful as it may seem, books by Himes have been printed and reprinted, sold and resold among publishers over the past thirty years—*and Himes has gotten virtually none of the money*! According to an interview with John A. Williams in *Amistad 1*, Chester Himes often does not know when his books are being published and republished in America. Having been broke most of his career, and in very ill health of late, he has been easy prey for the exploitive advance. Such was the situation with several of the Harlem series of detective novels. He wrote them quickly and sold them (or gave them away) just as quickly,

A Case of Rape

because he badly needed whatever money he could get. "I got a thousand dollar advance for each of my last three books," Himes told Williams.[1]

Another painful truth surrounding Himes's career is that, with rare exception, it has always been difficult to obtain any of Himes's books the first few months after their publication. Even the books that make the bestseller list—the hilariously satirical *Pinktoes* (1961), for example—are hard to come by. They go "out-of-stock, out-of-print," although they may still be on the bestseller list. I have been teaching courses in black literature for more than ten years. Every year when I order books by Chester Himes, I receive "out-of-stock, out-of-print" notices from the publishers. Similar to books by other black writers, one must too often search for Himes's books in stores that deal in "rare" books.

The fate of *If He Hollers Let Him Go* (1945) and *Lonely Crusade* (1947), foretold the fate of *Cast The First Stone* (1952), *The Third Generation* (1954) and *The Primitive* (1955). When *If He Hollers Let Him Go* was surging toward the bestseller list, a stop-print directive was issued by a female employee in the office of his own publisher. People were trying to buy the novel and could not get it because the bookstore orders were not being filled.

1. John A. Williams and Charles F. Harris, eds., *Amistad 1: Writings on Black History and Culture* (New York: Vintage Books, 1970), 30.

A Case of Rape

In his autobiography, *The Quality of Hurt*, Himes tells of another malignant act deliberately perpetrated against the book.

> [*If He Hollers Let Him Go*] was considered by the editorial committee for Doubleday Doran's *George Washington Carver Memorial Award* of twenty-five hundred dollars, but it was rejected because one of the women editors said it nauseated her. Instead, a novel called *Mrs. Palmer's Honey* was given the award. To add insult to injury, the advertising copy that appeared in the *Saturday Review of Literature* for *Mrs. Palmer's Honey* referred to my novel, *If He Hollers Let Him Go*, as a "series of epithets punctuated with spit." [2]

Obviously, to me at any rate, what enrages white people against Himes's books, particularly the woman who reacted so violently against *If He Hollers Let Him Go*, is the realistic manner in which black and white characters and relations are portrayed. In *If He Hollers*, a white woman who falsely accuses the black hero of raping her is depicted as she is—a racist white woman frustrated by her forbidden sexual desire for the black hero.

Malevolent deeds have also been perpetrated against books of Himes having nothing to do with black and white sex. A case in point is his second novel, *Lonely*

2. Chester Himes, *The Quality of Hurt*, vol. 1 of *The Autobiography of Chester Himes* (Garden City, New York: Doubleday & Company, Inc., 1972), 77.

A Case of Rape

Crusade, which centers around Lee Gordon, a black trade union organizer. Several promotional appearances scheduled for Himes in New York were cancelled at the last minute, without explanation, and the author and his work were harassed and maligned by various political factions in America, white and black.

In *The Quality of Hurt*, he reports on the manner in which *Lonely Crusade* was received.

> The communist review *The New Masses*, hit the stands with a vitriolic three-page attack by a black communist, headed by a silhouette of a black man carrying a white flag above a streamer saying "Himes carries the White Flag." *Ebony* magazine ran an editorial entitled "It Is Time To Count Your Blessings," to which it said: "The character Lee Gordon is psychotic, as is the author, Chester Himes." *The Atlantic Monthly* said: "Hate runs through this book like a streak of yellow bile." *Commentary*, a Jewish journal, ran a long diatribe . . . in which my book was compared to the "graffito on the walls of public toilets." . . . Willard Motley wrote a vicious personal attack charging me personally with statements taken from the dialogues of my characters. . . . The Communist Party had launched [a campaign] against bookstores that sold the book, by buying copies, damaging them, and taking them back to the stores and demanding their money back on the ground the book was trash. . . . The left hated it, the right hated it, Jews hated it, blacks hated it. . . . I think that what the great body of Americans most disliked was the fact I came too close to the truth.[3]

3. Ibid., 100-101.

A Case of Rape

In addition to problems with the distribution of his works and receipt of adequate compensation from publishers, Himes has also been plagued perennially by ill health, some of which could be due to his own mistakes and excesses, but a large measure of which could well be the result of damaging controversy persistently aimed at him and his works. Toward the end of chapter two in *The Quality of Hurt*, he writes:

> One will make more enemies by trying to be fair than by trying to tell the truth—no one believes it possible to tell the truth anyway—but it is just possible that you might be fair.[4]

An important source of controversy worth mentioning is the resentful attitudes that many black Americans, like their white counterparts, are prone to feel toward any black person who has lived outside of the United States for a length of time. When Himes returned from abroad to promote the publication of his autobiography, some blacks wanted to know if he was back "home" to stay for good. When he departed for Europe, disgruntled feelings were expressed throughout the rumor network of the black literary world. The fanfare and enthusiasm over him and the publication of his autobiography died instantly, like a candle flame exposed to sudden wind.

4. Ibid., 102.

A Case of Rape

Despite experiencing more than his share of deliberate evil and just plain old bad luck, Himes was published extensively in this country in the 1960s and early 1970s. Some of his literary creations made a tremendous popular impact that far outstripped the accomplishments of most novelists.

The nine Harlem detective novels—all of which are classed as "thrillers," featuring the colorful black detectives, Coffin Ed Johnson and Grave Digger Jones—include such American publication titles as: *A Rage In Harlem* (1964), *The Real Cool Killers* (1966), *Run, Man, Run* (1968), *All Shot Up* (1966), *The Heat's On* (1967), and *Blind Man With A Pistol* (1969). (*Blind Man* is the only one in the series originally published by an American publisher.)

When two of the detective novels were made into movies—"Cotton Comes to Harlem" and "Come Back Charleston Blue"—the works of Chester Himes gained popularity among the masses of movie-goers, and, consequently, among a wider variety of readers. It was during the windfall popularity from the movies (latter 1960s and early 1970s) that several of Himes's more "serious" works were reissued, notably *The Primitive*, *The Third Generation*, and *Pinktoes*. The two volumes of autobiography, *The Quality of Hurt* and *My Life of Absurdity*, were also published by American publishers in original hard-

A Case of Rape

back editions. Again, the reissued books, and the detective novels, plus the newly published autobiographies, went out-of-stock, out-of-print within a very short period of time. The present work, however, was not a part of what turned out to be a rather tumultuous but short-lived interest in Chester Himes.

A Case of Rape was written during 1956-57. It was first published in Paris in 1963 and entitled, *Une Affaire de Viol*. A second edition, *Affaire de Viol*, was issued in 1979. Both were produced by small French presses, Les Yeux Ouverts and Editions des Autres, respectively. It was not until 1980 that an American edition of the work was brought out by Targ Editions, a New York rare book publisher. The publication was limited, and the following statement appears on the last page:

> This first edition in English is limited to 350 copies, each signed by the author.

Obviously, the Targ Edition books are consigned to that great book fair in the sky known as "collector's items."

The Howard University Press publication of *A Case of Rape* marks the first time the book has been available in America on a large scale. Its publication is long overdue. It is not only a judicious service to Chester Himes but a great service to students and the general public, because it

A Case of Rape

singularly represents all of the elements constituting the quintessence of a theme that Himes has been hammering away at in a majority of his writings. It is a theme that is at once so historically rooted in race relations and yet so emotionally inflammable that we, both whites and blacks, have gone to maddening lengths to deny it as a fact of our lives and have made its acceptance a monumental taboo, seeking thereby to insulate ourselves against its existence. The fact is interracial love, occurring specifically and particularly between white women and black men. I call this fact, which appears as a major theme in the writings of Chester Himes, and all of the machinations surrounding it, *the scarlet equation*.

In other writings, but especially in several major works of fiction including, *If He Hollers Let Him Go*, *The Primitive*, and *Pinktoes*, Himes has laboriously dealt with this equation. His heavily autobiographical novel, *The Third Generation*, may also be considered a work in which the major portion deals with interracial love, in that Himes's real parents correspond to the mother and father in the novel. The mother is light-complexioned enough to be repeatedly mistaken for a white woman, and she "acts" like a white woman, while the father has pure negroid features and "acts" like a Negro, all of which provoke many problems. Indeed, I have heard some readers express the feeling that Himes has been inordinately preoc-

A Case of Rape

cupied with this theme. Chester Himes is a black man married to a white woman, and he has been privy to other black men/white women relationships. It seems altogether reasonable that he has been forced to deal with his more intimate knowledge of the scarlet equation, rather than with the white man/black woman equation.

Those of us who harbor a thoroughly ingrained repulsion toward interracial love, and we all are socialized in this way to some degree, find works dealing with this subject either mildly irritating or utterly disgusting. In large part, it has been Himes's apparent preoccupation with this theme that has figured in the controversial and often condemnatory reactions toward him. Some reactions have been so severe that it has been imputed that there is something "pathological" about Himes himself as a black man.

My view is that Himes's works constitute the most thoroughly illuminating "fictional" treatment available on one of the cardinal issues of our times: the tangled web of societal, institutional, and personal insanities surrounding the black man and the white woman. I submit that it is the existence of these insanities, so gothically depicted by Chester Himes, which we recognize within ourselves, that make us retaliate against Himes for daring to uncover them. These insanities, moreover, may very well lay at the bottom of the "nauseating" feelings and destructive

A Case of Rape

behavior toward Himes's books by certain whites in the publishing industry, as well as by some black people too.

The insanities may be collectively identified by two categories: the insanity of racism, and the insanity of sexism. According to the tenets of racism, the purpose of white people is to rule the world and blacks are here to serve whatever wishes whites might have. According to the tenets of sexism, the male mandate is to give guidance to, provide for, protect and dominate females. As racism applies to black people both male and female, sexism applies to women both white and black. It is my contention that in environments where racism and sexism are integral factors in the mores of a people, all associations between men and women of different races tend to suffer the entangled influences of both factors.

Whether by rape, subtle coercion, or mutual agreement, white men and black women have historically engaged in sexual relations with each other. Although these relationships have gone on and are going on, it is as if such relations are invisible. They are invisible because nobody seems to *want* to know about them.

On the other hand, the sensational publicity given to black man/white woman relationships suggests that interracial sex occurs in no other combination. Anyone can cite any number of contemporary black man/white woman marriages. But how many people can name five

A Case of Rape

black women who are married to white men? Why this is so, in the face of abundant evidence that such marriages exist, is a mystery, the unraveling of which might reveal more than anyone cares to deal with.

Whenever BLACK MAN/WHITE WOMAN is seen, mentioned or thought of, a red light flashes in our minds: The mere idea of sex between black men and white women is loaded with hot controversy. Black man/white woman association ignites emotions of pornography, nausea and repulsion; therefore, we are forced to deal with this association as the main priority. This is why I call black man/white woman relations the scarlet equation.

In most literature dealing with the scarlet equation the emphasis is placed on the impact of racism in these relationships, to the exclusion of sexism. Several works of Richard Wright—*Native Son, The Outsider* and *The Long Dream*—are cardinal examples. Other examples are *Night Song* by John A. Williams, *Soul on Ice* by Eldridge Cleaver, and *Another Country* by James Baldwin. But when sexism is so obviously a salient ingredient of the subject under consideration, to ignore it or misname it is to short-change our understanding. Even though Himes does not employ the word sexism in the narrative of *A Case of Rape*, in describing the forces that have victimized Elizabeth Hancock he uses the term *inverted racism*. Before she met Scott Hamilton, Elizabeth had not been

A Case of Rape

victimized because of her race. She had been victimized because of her sex.

To wit, in *A Case of Rape*, Himes explores the *racism* and *sexism* of interracial love and shows that when they occur together, the two factors mask each other and are virtually inseparable. In Scott Hamilton's personality, there are effects of the insanities he experienced from having lived in a racist and sexist society. Likewise, Elizabeth's personal history attests to her victimization by the sexist insanities of her cultural background and by her husband. In fact, all of the black men in the novel, as well as the white woman, are victims of the racism and sexism of Western society.

The accused men and Elizabeth's husband, are in possession of information that cold have mitigated the conviction of the men and could possibly have exonerated them. The central question, then, becomes why and how were the four men convicted when there was evidence that could have supported their innocence? What made their conviction possible?

After the opening overview, the majority of *A Case of Rape* is devoted to unraveling the details leading to the rape-murder conviction of innocent men following the strange death of Elizabeth Hancock. Since there is no eyewitness to the alleged crime, the details consist of circumstantial evidence surrounding four black men associating with a white woman. The men then are convicted by the circumstantial evidence for being black and associating with a white woman. While black men associating with a white woman is not a legal offense, it is a social taboo. To break it carries social disapprobation equalling that reserved for the crime with which they are charged. In the minds of whites, black men/white women friendships constitute an extra-legal (or supra-legal) crime of implied sexual intercourse and therefore of rape. Notice how the rape charge is stressed throughout the trial rather than the murder question. Ironically, this emphasis is not only normal in a racist society but is perpetuated by the irrational animosities arising from the mere thought of an affair between a white woman and four black men. Indeed, the opening chapters of the book serve to set the stage for Himes to depict and expound throughout the remainder on the deranging effects of racism and sexism, both on the level of individual personality and on the societal level, as writ large in black man/white woman relationships.

The choice of setting in Paris functions as a sort of clinical laboratory for Himes's meticulous study. Both the romantic aura of desperate love between Scott and Elizabeth and the uncanny effects of racism on their relationship are intensified and heightened against the backdrop of the supposedly liberal Parisian environment. The Parisian setting also highlights the fugitive stigmata that all

A Case of Rape

racist societies stamp upon interracial lovers. Almost universally, black men/white women associating together are seen as "fugitives" from both the white world and the black world. For example, in extremely racist environments, interracial couples actually hide from other people. In less bigoted situations they are nevertheless fearful and tend to engage in certain avoidance tactics. They appear to be forever in flight—psychological flight and geographical flight as well.

Moreover, the fugitive motif—the motif of exile and alienation—invades the individual lives and personalities of Elizabeth Hancock and her four alleged rapists. All had left America, their native home, and are residing in a foreign land, or rather, they are "floating around" in a foreign land, wearing the label of the "expatriate." They have departed from the mores of their culture, since those mores have oppressed and demeaned them, but at the same time they still bear the scars of their degradation. Both collectively and individually, they are haunted by the sense of guilt their native culture has imposed upon them, and they are irritated by their sure knowledge of being oddities in a foreign culture. Borne in their own consciousnesses, these stigmata—of being fugitives, of being "renegades" from society—bring the fivesome together as kindred souls, as wounded people seeking healing and desiring love and companionship far more than

121

A Case of Rape

merely sex. Paradoxically, and yet quite naturally, the situation brings about their condemnation. Condemnation? Yes, because no matter what the circumstances, above all else, the supreme taboo of the world is that black men and white women are not supposed to associate with, let alone love one another. If they do, it's an automatic crime.

Himes spends considerable time delineating the backgrounds of Elizabeth and each of the four men in terms of the formative ingredients of their personalities, their genealogies, how they happened to end up in Paris, and what they were like before coming to know each other. Himes does this to show that once we have been victimized, we carry the effects in our psyches. Once we are poisoned by the venom of sexism and racism, it becomes almost impossible for us to relate to one another as healthy persons, even in an environment relatively free of the poison.[5] Every situation involving blacks and whites, especially where male and female are concerned, is liable to be misperceived, stereotyped, and misconstrued.

Scott and Elizabeth wanted so desperately to love each other, perhaps *too* desperately. The healing that both Scott and Elizabeth sought in and through their relation-

5. For a more elaborate explanation of this assertion, see Calvin Hernton, *Sex and Racism in America* (New York: Grove Press, Inc., 1965). See especially chapters two and three.

A Case of Rape

ship was affected by the very sexist and racist mythologies surrounding relationships between black men and white women that, first and foremost, they had to overcome in themselves. Because while they thought they knew each other, what they saw were but socially inflicted distortions of their true selves.

The tangled web of sexual racism involves a tragic irony and a cruel dialectic. Here, the four black men's show of deference to Elizabeth was not rooted in solid ground. It sprang from their bad feelings about being outcasts of humanity, and from their internalization of the white man's own "chivalrous" idolatry of the "lily white lady." Himes writes, "They all were Negroes who revered cultured American white women, desired them, perhaps, in a dreamlike manner." It was for these reasons, these feelings, that in the emotional eyes of the four men, Elizabeth was not a mere woman but was a kind of magical object whose friendship the men believed would conjure up in them a sense of pride and self-worth as men.

Elsewhere I have written that the denial of the black man's humanity is in large measure predicated by the existence of the white world's racist perspective. By this anomalous standard, the black world is described as dirty, savage, sinful. The white world is supposed to be virtuous, holy, chaste, at the center of which stands the white woman. According to the mythology of white suprem-

123

acy, it is the white woman who is the "immaculate conception" of Western civilization; the possession of her is therefore perceived as a sort of ontological affirmation of the black man's self-worth. On a deeper level, however, if not consciously then subconsciously, the black man is aware of his devalued humanity compared to the overblown valuation of white women. Mixed up with his desire to possess her, and his adoration for her, there is often an irritating bitterness, guilt, and even hatred. Of Shelly Russell and Ted Elkins, Himes writes: "Deep inside of Shelly's reverence for this type of white woman, there was an animosity as deep as Ted's own."

To further explain their behavior, Himes notes that all the men, except for Caesar Gee, showed signs of having complexes regarding the white ancestry in their genealogies. Ted Elkins, for example, hated his white grandfather and felt ashamed of his mother's illegitimacy. Yet he dated and married white women. Shelly Russell maintained reverence for all the attributes of upper class, cultured Americans that his white wife possessed. "Consequently," writes Himes, "he had a sort of reverence for all women who were her prototypes." Even Caesar Gee, whose heritage was pure African, and who did not like white American women, nevertheless engaged in relations with French and, presumably, other European white women; his paintings showed an inordinate preoccupation with black

A Case of Rape

and white sex of a "pornographic" nature. The great Roger Garrison himself "felt inferior to and ill at ease in the presence of American white women of Mrs. Hancock's heritage." Altogether, the men were similarly affected by the insanities inherent in the racist and sexist societies in which they were born and had lived.

The four black men brought these feelings and experiences to their encounter with the "cultured" white woman. Thus, the reverence they all held for her was frought with the desperation and misconceptions of rejected men, and had very little basis in reality. For, as Himes tells us, they did not know, and perhaps were incapable of knowing, the real Elizabeth.

On the other hand, *A Case of Rape* shows that the perspective from which Elizabeth viewed these men, which was a human one, was, nevertheless, also blind. Elizabeth's background and upbringing had sheltered her not only from the realities of her own world but from those of the black world as well. Elizabeth believed that all black men were kind to white women without any knowledge of the emotional brew of love-and-hate simmering beneath that show of kindness. She truly thought, for example, that Scott was a "complete person." She even thought her husband was a complete person! She knew nothing of Scott's deep-seated insecurities and knew nothing of the thin-skinned pettiness to which he and the others, including Roger Garrison, were all susceptible. As Chester Himes tells the reader, Elizabeth was a "casualty of white Christian society," reared according to the self-flagellating ethics of Puritanism, and socialized to be "feminine"—to be soft, weak, dependent, and therefore easily victimized. Thus, she had been kept ignorant of the dehumanizing forces of both sexism and racism even as she floated back and forth between the reality of her own world and that of her black lover.

In specific references to Scott and Elizabeth, Himes writes that they "were not too far apart in race, upbringing, or religion. They had the same traditions, the same moral outlook, the same disappointments by goodness and God." Thus, although classified as a Negro, the inner fibre of Scott Hamilton, similar to that of Elizabeth, was ridden with insecurity, ignorance, and blindness. Himes tells the reader that it never occurred to Scott that Elizabeth "was as much a casualty of racism as himself," but it was "an inverted sort of racism that perpetuates the dominance of the male." Indeed, Scott puts on the garb of the "knight in shining armour" to rescue his "lady in distress." "As a consequence," writes Himes, "from the first to the last, his love for her was but a dream, acting itself out in his mind. . . . The real Elizabeth he never saw and never knew."

Collectively, the four defendants, as well as Roger Gar-

A Case of Rape

rison, show that they are held hostage by the interplay of the racist and sexist elements within themselves. Tragically, they are not aware of this. The men harbor all kinds of petty grudges and jealousies toward each other, apart from any reference to their appreciation for the white woman who became a symbol of their alter-egos. Further, the friendship of the men is based largely on the artificiality of race, since they come together as expatriates who are all subject to racist victimization. Their bonding, therefore, easily turns into manhood rivalry and conflict. The emotional fibres of the men are so thin and insecure that the most insignificant thing becomes of the utmost importance to them. This is also true in America, where daily we hear of black men killing each other following some petty argument. For the most part, the male characters in Himes's story do indeed unconsciously—and often as a socially induced pattern of relating between males—victimize each other. This tendency may also be heightened by the effects of racism on the masculine psychology, which is a competitive, "I'm-a-better-man-than-you" psychology.

To those who are unaware of the customs of men, especially men in sexist and racist environments, the notion of fooling around with the Spanish Fly occurs in the lifetime of nearly every male in Western society, usually during adolescence. Stories about the mythological effects

127

A Case of Rape

of Spanish Fly on women become a part of the ideal masculine sexual fantasy—you give it to females and it makes them do wild things. In *A Case of Rape*, we learn that Elizabeth's husband customarily used Spanish Fly to prepare her for a night of sex. An analogy can be made between the reference to "The Great American Myth"— the notion that black men can fuck, white women in particular, longer, harder, and better than any other men—and Spanish Fly. Remember, it was a white American reporter who gave the substance to Scott in the first place and who remarked about the great myth. Both of them, black men and Spanish Fly, can drive women crazy. Also recall it was Ted Elkins who secretly wished to give the bottle of Spanish Fly to Elizabeth and steer her in the direction of Caesar Gee, whom Elkins fancied she thought of as an ape. Elkins "wanted to see how she, in a state of sexual excitement, would respond to an ape."

In other works, *If He Hollers Let Him Go* for example, Himes also dwelled on the theme of black men being falsely accused of rape. This is true of Richard Wright's classic novel, *Native Son*, and John O. Killens's *Youngblood*. It is also definitely addressed in Angela Davis's study, *Women, Race and Class*. In black literature in general this theme is a central one. This is why the title of *A Case of Rape* is loaded with significance. In fact, *A Case of Rape* is not about an actual rape. Rather, it is about

A Case of Rape

the mythology of rape as associated with the historical stereotype of black men being rapists of white women. The mythology of rape is another one of the sexist-racist insanities that grew out of slavery to justify keeping black men and women in bondage. I am not saying that black men do not rape. But the mythology of black men as rapists of white women serves to incite all white people against the entire black struggle for equality by charging that all black men really want is to sleep with the daughters of white men. Moreover, since white civilization has made the white woman a goddess, all attempts by blacks to gain any rights whatever are viewed as "rape attacks" against the white supremacist world. I have termed this phenomenon the sexualization of racism. The definition of all black men as rapists also serves as a distraction from the white man's crime and guilt of rape committed against black and white women, both during and since slavery. It also projects the blame onto black men for these crimes.

Thus, the four black men were convicted of the "crime" of associating with a fetish of the white racist-sexist world. In the twisted minds and emotions of white racists, any "nigger" associating with the "precious" woman is automatically guilty of rape, whether he actually commits it or not. This—the symbolic, circumstantially imaginary rape, which is altogether real to the racist—is what *A Case of Rape* is about.

A Case of Rape

Yet, the book most certainly concerns actual rape. It concerns the white man's rape of Elizabeth Hancock, and the white world's sexist victimization of women, in general. Elizabeth, moreover, had been "raped" all of her life by Christian hypocrisy and Puritan degradation of the female sex. She had been socialized in the belief that sex was pleasurable for men only. She had never experienced an orgasm and was ignorant of the most rudimentary knowledge relating to sex, her own sexuality in particular.

Himes writes that Elizabeth was "one of those unfortunate victims of a code of ethics promulgated by the white race as its own private doctrine for the elevation of whites only; a code of ethics which the white race has been the only race to reject." Like women in general, she was cast in the traditional role of an object to be dominated and exploited by men. Her husband, for example, performed "surgery" on her for sexual purposes; he actually felt that she enjoyed having pain inflicted on her. She produced babies and remained loyal for a time to her puritanical indoctrination.

The husband, André Brissaud, raped and mutilated Elizabeth in mind and soul, as well. He drove her to a nervous breakdown and carted her off to an asylum. He pimped Elizabeth, took her inheritance and purchased himself a plush dental practice. The clincher is the way in which he regarded her: "He felt her to be a possession,

A Case of Rape

and he was never any more tender toward her than toward any of his other possessions, his dog or his car."

At this juncture, it is important to point out how Stella Browning, the one black woman in *A Case of Rape*, is presented in contrast to the saintly image of Elizabeth Hancock. Himes describes her as a "black haired piece of red hot sex, rotten to the core. . . . [She was] working as an amateur whore and sleeping free with three men." Her only saving trait is that "she had a voice." Scott married her (she was seventeen!) because she was a "challenge" or perhaps as "revenge against his white ancestors." Scott never loved or respected her. He was ashamed of her background and viewed her with contempt. On the other hand, Scott instantly falls in love with the white paragon of virtue, whom he calls "Lisbeth," and to whom he declares, "I knew you were the one person in the world for me." He even uses the money Stella sends him to finance his love affair with "Lisbeth."

Though she is never brought to life as a person or a character, in my view Stella Browning is a dynamite and wholesome woman. Unlike Scott and the rest of the characters, including Elizabeth, Stella has her feet on the solid ground of reality. She is free of the personality hangups and middle-class pretentiousness of Scott and his cronies. In a society that is doubly hard on black women, Stella's independence has been earned through what ordinary

A Case of Rape

black people call "the school of hard knocks." But she is given no credit. Stella Browning is not only relegated to the proverbial "back burner" by Scott's insane, angelic perception of Elizabeth. The black woman's denigration is implied by the hyperbolic significance attributed to the black man/white woman relationship—a significance fueled by the myth of the black man's alleged desire to rape white women. Unfortunately, it is this myth which motivates Roger Garrison in his misguided investigation.

It takes no microscope to see that Roger seems more afflicted with the same disease of racist victimization and the resultant paranoia that is the anguish of the four black men he seeks to exonerate. He carries an added burden of being the one and only American Negro who is recognized on a world scale as a literary genius, a sort of overblown "Native Son" living in exile. So bloated is he with his own sense of importance that petty, even silly emotionalisms prevent him from solving the case, and cause him to contribute to the demise of his four compatriates and to that of Elizabeth as well, by sending that letter to her publisher!

Notice the role that spite and malice assume in the lives of all the "victims." Sheldon Russell married his first white wife in retaliation against the racism he experienced at Harvard University. Scott Hamilton married Stella, a black *cafe au lait*-complexioned woman, as revenge against

A Case of Rape

his own white ancestry. Ted Elkins gave the bottle of poisonous sherry to Elizabeth out of "unpremeditated, racially-inspired spite"; and Roger Garrison had sent the letter also out of "racially-inspired" spite. When Elizabeth learned of the letter that was sent to her publisher, she was shattered to know she had such spiteful enemies.

It is significant that Chester Himes, in nearly all his works, writes from his own experience, basing many of his fictional characters on the lives of real people. Although I have not found any case having occurred in France such as that described in *A Case of Rape*, I have no doubt that the book is based more on reality than make-believe. In fact, a significant portion of Chester Himes's autobiography deals with his European affair with an aristocratic white woman, Alva Trent Van Olden Barneveldt. The details of this affair are strikingly recognizable as those depicted in *A Case of Rape*.

Likewise, the character Roger Garrison is reminiscent of the writer Richard Wright, who figures importantly in the autobiography. Wright occupied a place of unprecedented eminence in the minds of both blacks and whites the world over, although self-exiled in Paris for almost two decades until his death in 1960.

Even as far-fetched as the story might seem, the Spanish Fly incident is not purely fictional. According to Michel Fabre, who translated the 1979 French edition of *A Case*

A Case of Rape

of Rape, Himes authenticated the existence of such a case as having occurred in Columbus, Ohio, in 1929, involving a professor at Ohio State University and a student who died as a result of having been given Spanish Fly.[6] Himes also employed a variation on the same theme in one of his earlier novels, *Cast The First Stone* (1952). Ergo, as Fabre noted, Chester Himes has a great facility for "transforming historical events into imaginary episodes; he is masterful at basing fictional situations on everyday happenings."

A Case of Rape reads like a blend of a case study, a court clerk's report, a journalist's report, a thriller-mystery novel, an essay, and a moral tract. Accordingly, students of literature might experience some confusion in determining the genre of the book. The matter may be cleared up when we take into account that Himes had intended to compose a much longer, more thorough work. According to Fabre, Himes referred to the book we have here as his synopsis of *A Case of Rape*, in a letter to his friend and translator, Yves Malartic. The book Himes planned was to be a "Dostoievskian [sic] work . . . several volumes." This, no doubt, would have been an incredible project. But the full-scale narrative was never written.

6. Michel Fabre, "Dissecting Western Pathology: A Critique—*A Case of Rape*," *Black World* (March, 1972). Other Fabre quotes and references are from the same article.

A Case of Rape

The reader should be glad to know that the present work is typical Chester Himes, even though it only sketches a much larger concept. It bears the Himesian trademark for exact detail, quick wit, and an astute ability for presenting complex elements in a thriller-mystery narrative. Most of all, there is within these pages the aesthetics of a profound moral conscience. It says that Truth, no matter how unpleasant or taboo, is the ultimate beauty of a work of art. This, of course, leads to the controversy that is nearly always generated by Himes's works.

Specifically, in *A Case of Rape*, Himes deals daringly, bluntly, with the forbidden, red-light subject of the scarlet equation. While he unravels the racist and sexist elements in the social backgrounds and personalities of the men and the woman, and deals forthrightly with the motives leading to their involvement, he equally tackles the inhumanity and downright insanity of a morally and sexually degenerate world where a white woman senselessly loses her life and four black men are wrongly condemned.

It is significant that Himes portrays André Brissaud both as an individual and as a representative of the entire decadence of white civilization. Personally and symbolically, he is depicted as the epitome of the white man's inhumanity to women—and to men. On page 76, Himes writes:

A Case of Rape

He was imbued with an ingrown, refined evil of generations of decadence; an evil distilled form the dark superstitions of countless centuries of Christian expedience and aged in the slowly rotting *bien faite* culture of blasé and jaded city. His was an ungodly evil that was all the more terrible because he didn't know it was evil. An evil that had been in existence for so long it had attained another status, termed by the Americans as *continental.*

The depth and scope of Brissaud's evil is brought home by his collaboration with the Nazi Wehrmacht regime.

When it comes to Brissaud's role in the condemnation of the four men, I am reminded of the novel, *Sport of The Gods,* by Paul Laurence Dunbar, America's foremost "controversial" nineteenth century black poet. In the novel, a northern white man comes south to visit the plantation of his aristocratic, slave-holding brother. Pretending to be a financial success, the man is actually penniless. While visiting his brother, he steals a sum of his brother's money. Of course, the black handyman is accused, tried, and sentenced to a long term in prison. The white man, who is of the Christian faith, could have exonerated the Negro with little consequence to himself. But he refused to do so, letting the black man take the rap for his crime, which leads to the demise of the black man's family, to say nothing of his own imprisonment.

Similarly, Brissaud represents not only white civiliza-

A Case of Rape

tion's practice of blaming its crimes on black people. He also is a psychological reflection of white people's inability to extend fairness to black men and women. How can you be fair to those you seek to oppress, exploit, and vilify? When Brissaud finds out that his wife has been lover to a black man during their separation, Brissaud became more excited about possessing her sexually than he was about reconciling the broken marriage. At the same time he felt it would blemish his character as a white man to come to the defense of Negroes accused of the rape-murder of his wife. What would people think of him as a white man? What would he think of himself? If he told the truth to save the black men, revealing that his former wife and mother of his daughters had been intimate with a black man, it would cause intolerable shame on himself and his daughters as well. What white man or woman would blame him for his silence?

But if the psychology of white men as oppressors is insanely weird, so is the psychology that has been wrought in black men over three centuries of oppression. Black men are afflicted with the mentality of victims, they have the feelings and emotions of the damned. Therefore, although the defendants were intelligent, even intellectual men, they had the emotional and mental reflex of all true victims—paranoia! Or, as Himes phrases it, "pure, unadulterated fear."

A Case of Rape

Automatically, the men understood that no matter what they said or did, they would not be believed, especially because they were innocent. But how could they have been innocent? They were black. Were they not guilty of breaking the most sacrosanct of taboos—being with a white woman? Even black people themselves would feel a conscientiousness to condemn them: "Niggers shouldn't have been hanging out with that white bitch, no way." Their crime was their color and their sex. Their crime was also their oppression. Since oppressors strive to make their victims feel responsible for their predicament, and since blackness is viewed by whites as a crime, the men felt guilty indeed, and were presumed guilty by everyone.

The unfairness Chester Himes has experienced throughout his life, specifically from the publishing world and from critics and readers, is the same injustice experienced by Elizabeth and the four men, which altogether belongs to the terrible category of "man's inhumanity to man" that Himes addresses on the final page of the book. After all, Shelly and Ted conspired to give the bottle containing the Spanish Fly to Elizabeth as Scott's back was turned. Envy, jealousy, and a feeling of having been wronged by Scott and Elizabeth were the sources of their racially inspired, spiteful feelings toward Elizabeth and Scott, particularly because they were lovers. Even more revealing is

A Case of Rape

that Scott Hamilton could not face having it known that his former lover, Elizabeth, had informed him of having been sexually exhausted by her former husband a few hours prior to her and Scott's rendezvous. Scott feared what people would think of him. What role had he played in the whole affair? Would he be thought a homosexual? Anyway, he feared, and knew, that people would not believe Elizabeth had visited her former husband, and he could not prove it. Who, moreover, would believe the truth of why Elizabeth was in the room with four black men? What could black men and white women possibly have in common except lust? What, anyway, would possess these men to desire to prove their dignity and honesty to this white woman, and reassure her that none of them had sent the damaging letter? Who would believe that Elizabeth found in these black men a kindred spirit, trusted them implicitly, and felt infinitely safe with them? No one. The prosecutor himself found these claims "childish and insincere," mere excuses to lure the woman into an orgy.

The men "could not conceive of a white jury believing their innocence," and rightly so. Herein lies the ultimate import of the title: *A Case of Rape* reveals a tragically ironic metaphor of rape. For the minds and emotions of the four black men were raped—just as the bodies and minds and emotions of all black people have been raped

139

A Case of Rape

by centuries of "man's inhumanity to man." The ultimate effect of oppression is to have the victims collaborate in their own oppression. This is why Scott and his buddies could not come forward with the truth. The men, "had been [utterly] conditioned by their culture, by the preconceptions and generalizations of the white race which always attributes the crimes of one Negro to the entire Negro race," until they simply had been rendered incapable of believing that anyone would believe the truth. If they testified that Ted had given Elizabeth the Spanish Fly out of spite, it would have been tantamount to confessing they all were accomplices. "No one," writes Himes, "would believe they had not actually raped her." In the last line of the book, Himes lays the blame where it ultimately belongs: "We are all guilty."

Himes's masterful writing, and especially his indomitable sense of the morality of truth and fairness, reveal the integrity and frailty of the human being beneath all of the artificial trappings of society, which form the insightful substructure of this work. Because of these attributes, *A Case of Rape* will be relevant for as long as human life is relevant.

Oberlin, Ohio
1984